Veiled Murder – What other people say…

"This book held my interest from beginning to end. I could not guess who the murderer was, though (in good mystery-writing format) the clues were there. A touch of murder, a touch of mystery, and a touch of romance! All woven together magnificently!"

~ Connie Wehmeyer

"Great first book! Not only a murder mystery, but a close look at family relationships."

~ Penny Cutler

"Intriguing characters. Love the ladies on the porch! Tenroc is a very promising new author. Can't wait to read more."

~Gloria Garrett

"Murder, mystery, sinister women, love, this story has it all. The author captivated me with unexpected twists and turns."

~Patricia Hoover

Veiled Murder

MIA TENROC

VEILED MURDER by Mia Tenroc
© 2016 Mia Tenroc.
ISBN: 978-1-944433-00-0

McToner Publishing Inc.
P.O. Box 37
Goldenrod, Florida 32722
McTonerPublishing@gmail.com
www.Miatenroc.com

Permissions:
© Timonko|Dreamstime.com
© Irochka|Dreamstime.com
© Roz Boris|Dreamstime.com

Cover layout:
Rik Feeney / usabookcoach@gmail.com

DEDICATION

This book is dedicated to all the in-laws that suffered due to bad influences by their daughter-in-law. I want to thank the 4 women and 2 men that shared their true life experiences with me even though it was an emotional journey. This book is for you and in it you win.

ACKNOWLEDGMENTS

I would like to add a special thank you to my good friends that encouraged me to follow my passion of writing, helped by reviewing my work, and giving me great ideas.

GROUP OF FRIENDS

"I can't take it anymore! We need to be in harmony, in sync!" Josephine understood and suggested they both start the rocking chairs in the back position. Jean then said, "One, two, three, go!" Josephine and her sister, Jean, began to rock back and forth together. Before, it had been hard to talk with one being forward and one being back. The sisters were both a little bit of a perfectionist that way.

Jean loved the home in which she currently lived. It was more than 100 years old and built by their great-grandfather. Their grandfather also helped on the construction crew of the Friend's Home. The Home was a huge three-story white house with a wrap-around porch on three sides. The building was for seniors that could no longer live on the farms or didn't want to live alone, kind of the forerunner of the senior living towers built today.

The men had their rooms on the top floor, the women had their rooms on the second floor, and the first floor contained the common areas. There was a library for reading, a social room for watching TV and playing games, and a dining room for eating and socializing. The kitchen was out back, connected to the house by a breezeway. In the olden days, the area was populated by mostly farmers and fishermen that worked hard for their money and never had much of it. The Home gave them somewhere to live and a sense of community when they could no longer work. The Home was built before Social Security existed. The church elders understood the need to help those no longer in the best of health that needed a place to live comfortably.

The residents were permitted to live in the Home for the amount of their Social Security check. In exchange, the Home provided cleaning service, meals, and sometimes entertainment. Unlike modern retirement facilities, the Home did not charge any additional monthly fees, thus whatever money the residents had before entering as residents or from other sources was theirs to keep. The Home was not modern, but being surrounded with history was more important to those that lived there. The fact that their great-grandfather built this work of art made Josephine and Jean celebrities to the residents.

Each resident had a private sitting room, bedroom, and bathroom. The size was mostly 12 by 12 feet on each of the two rooms, big enough to live comfortably. The residents were permitted to keep a car. Like family, residents that owned cars would offer to drive for residents that had no transportation for shopping trips or to visit their families.

The other reason the sisters were considered celebrities was they had assisted in solving a large number of murders, even though they were never detectives or with the police. It was just something they stumbled upon throughout their lives. The pair also traveled extensively, with Josephine often visiting Europe and Jean having been to all 50 states and parts of Canada. Thus, if they weren't telling stories of murder, they were recounting their travel adventures as part of the late morning entertainment. The porch was often filled during the late morning hour with not just residents, but neighbors and friends as well.

Today, the sisters were surrounded by their water aerobics buddies, Belinda, Eve, and Priscilla. Belinda was a very successful marketing executive before her retirement. She has a personality that bubbles with positive words and wise advice. She lives in the largest house in this small town, which she inherited from her parents. Eve possesses a great sense of humor even though she worries and frets over many things. She lives in a small house on 3rd Street a couple of doors down from Josephine and her husband. Eve is on her fifth marriage, which is only successful because her hoarder husband lives on a farm while she lives in town. Even though she bought a small house intending to live alone, her granddaughter recently moved in with her. Priscilla, who lived in the room next to Jean at the Friend's Home, was quiet and didn't talk much, making her the best listener of the group. She pays careful attention to what is being said and has a unique way of asking pertinent questions to enlighten the conversation. She truly is an interesting person, but is so humble she doesn't realize her contribution to discussions really matters.

While the ladies were rocking in their chairs enjoying their ice tea, the peace and quiet was suddenly disturbed by the loud honking of horns and shouts of joy. Leaving the church from across the street was a wedding party. Jean frowned and her muscles grew tight but she didn't say a word. Priscilla noticed the sudden change from the happy conversation that was occurring. Josephine kept on talking and was ignoring her sister.

Priscilla asked Jean, "What's wrong? Why the change in mood?"

Josephine said "She gets like that at weddings.

Just keep talking and she will relax and join in again." Priscilla had a look of concern and curiosity.

Jean said "I just don't like weddings."

Not taking the hint, Priscilla kept pressing for an explanation.

Jean confessed, "Even though I have been to probably a hundred beautiful weddings, including those of my own children, the sights and sounds of a wedding will always take me back to a wedding where a murder occurred."

"What?" shouted a shocked Priscilla.

The others broke from their conversations and joined Priscilla in trying to learn more about this murder from their friend. "You mean someone died at a wedding?"

"Two died that day, one literally and one figuratively." Jean finally whispered. She knew she was trapped at this point. The others would never give up the questioning until she told the story. "The Bride was murdered. The groom became estranged from family and friends, ending up alone. I'll tell the story, but in the usual third-person format with all names changed to protect the innocent." Jean started all of her stories with this disclaimer. "The story I'm about to tell is fictional, and any resemblance to anyone living or dead is purely coincidental."

The listeners knew there was probably as much truth to the story as there was fiction, but told in a manner to avoid hurting anyone. Therefore, names, locations, and some events were changed, but the stories nevertheless kept everyone riveted and were considered much more entertaining than watching a movie or television show.

CHAPTER 1 - THE BRIDE

The room was a nice size, with beige wallpaper containing roses spaced throughout. There was no bed even though this had been a bedroom of someone with wealth. Sitting at the 1920 vanity with the leaded glass mirror, Doreen Sanchez was smiling and thinking this beautiful old home they rented was perfect for her wedding day. She was 26-years-old, so it was about time she got married. Doreen was brought up to believe that you got married right after high school and started producing babies right away. She could never understand why no one wanted to marry her. She was 5-foot 2-inches, petite, and had a pretty heart-shaped face with her nose turned up just right. She considered herself very pretty, so what was there not to love? She felt the type of wealth the house displayed should have belonged to her every day, not just rented for this one event. She hoped her husband could someday provide her with comforts she deserved.

Doreen had to act all her life to give the impression that she liked being with her family. She tried to fool others into believing she was a wonderful person. Even in her wedding dress, she felt a need to practice her faces because today would be the biggest show of all. Time for the practice to begin. She tilted her head down, lifting her eyes similar to the shy Princess Diana look, expressing sincere innocence. She practiced pouting to convey sadness that could easily be made a happy face with the right word. She did her "woe is me look" when she turned her head to the right and lifted her chin up. Her hand would be on her chest placed above the breast and below the neck. She used this face when she wanted to play the martyr. Next, she put on the happy face where she would look up, smile and shake her head, playfully tossing her hair. The "I really care what you are saying" look, even though she could care less, was a straight face with no emotion and wide eyes. She had a whole series of faces that got her through every situation. She had it all so carefully planned. Today, she planned to drive the final stake between her husband-to-be and his mom so no one would interfere with her taking control of him. Her mother taught her well about the importance of control.

After all, Maria didn't have control over her

first husband, Doreen's real father, and he ended up leaving the family. Her step-father, a man that Doreen considered her "real father," was willing to give his wife everything she wanted. Maria limited her husband's visits with his family to twice a year and only at Maria's two bedroom, one bath, 24 by 30 foot shack to keep total control of interaction with his family. His famous line was, "Give your mother what she wants. She's going to get it anyway and it saves us from living through the hell we would go through if we refuse." Maria loved that line and would smile happily when it was said.

Doreen's concentration broke with the sound of her mother berating her first-born daughter Dolly. "You need to stand up straighter and keep the wrap over your shoulders to hide those fat arms," scolded Maria. Dolly looked a lot like Doreen if it wasn't for the weight. Unfortunately, the cute turned-up nose was more like a pig's snout with the additional pounds. Doreen really liked the fact that Dolly was the whipping child in the family. Maybe because she was created out of wedlock, and Maria was angry about the failed marriage to their father. The reality was Maria was a negative person with only so many kind words to go around, so the three sisters were always pitted against each other for attention and approval.

Maria always told them she selected names that

started with a DO so they would be her "do, do, do girls." Do what I want, do it when I want, do it how I want, and we'll all be happy, was her favorite catch line. The girls knew it wasn't worth the effort to do anything else. Maria even helped Doreen plot how to alienate Andrew's family so Doreen could run her household the same as her mother.

The youngest sister, Donna, had just completed doing Doreen's hair and makeup and was changing into her bridesmaid dress. The three sisters looked very much alike, except Donna was taller and willowy instead of short and curvy. Donna was clearly the mom's favorite, so poor middle child Doreen had to get time and attention when she could. Being the first sister to marry was a feather in her cap. Marrying someone with a good education and income also won her favors. Donna had a knack for selecting losers that didn't meet her mother's approval. It was nice of Donna to offer to do Doreen's hair for her perfect day. Doreen was worried that Donna would be jealous of the attention Doreen would receive.

Suddenly, a scream came from her mother. "Doreen, get in here immediately!"

The last thing Doreen wanted was her mother's anger to ruin the day. "What is it, Mother? Are you okay?"

Maria slapped Doreen and pointed to the yard.

"Who invited him? Did you do it?"

Doreen looked to where her mother was pointing but didn't recognize the man. "Who is it, Mother?"

Maria retorted, "Don't act cute with me. You know that is your father!"

Doreen had not seen her father for 15 years. Besides aging, she had been so young when he left she didn't remember much about him. "Are you sure?" she whispered.

"Dolly," shouted Maria, "get down there and tell him he isn't welcome and to leave immediately."

Doreen started to cry. This day was not going well. The weather appeared gloomy for an outdoor wedding, her mother was seething, and now there was a red imprint of her mother's hand on her cheek showing. Donna rushed to her side and brought her back to the dressing table, helping to comfort Doreen, and getting out make-up to repair the damage.

Dolly went downstairs and approached the man who was almost a stranger to her. "Are you my father, Juan?" she asked timidly.

"Dolly, I'm so glad to see you," he said with sincerity.

"How did you know about this and how did you find us?" questioned Dolly.

"Doreen's husband contacted me and said he thought Doreen missed me. He said since so much time had passed since I left, that things would be fine for me to be here. I didn't think so, and I can tell by your face it isn't. Do you want me to leave?"

Dolly, looking over her shoulder to the window where she knew her mother was watching, explained Maria's reaction.

Juan said, "Walk me to the car and tell your mom you wanted to make sure I got in and drove away. The reason why I stayed away all these years is your mother attacked me with a knife. The police didn't believe me because I restrained her wrists, causing bruises. Your mother and one of her sisters said I beat Maria all the time, which was a lie. I was told if Maria wanted to press charges, I could go to jail. Maria cut a deal that if I disappeared forever, she would drop the charges. What could I do? I could only hope she was a better mom to you girls than she was as a wife to me."

Juan slipped Dolly a business card in such a way no one would see. "Here is my number. Don't give it to her, but if you want to contact me, you're an adult now, I will be there for you. If you don't contact me, I understand. I would love to give you a kiss on the head but I'm sure we are being watched, so just point at the car."

Dolly pointed as if giving a command to leave and her father got in and drove away. He drove out of her life again. She wondered if he really was sincere about contacting him. It seemed like he was, so she put the card into her bra before turning and waving to her mother.

Dolly, trying not to cry, returned to the room and into her mother's open arms. "What a great job you did, Dolly. I'm proud of you. It's almost time for the wedding to begin so we need to finish getting ready."

Doreen was so angry at Andrew and planned to let him know how displeased she was later. She let him think he had some rights and some say in their relationship because being too bossy too fast might drive him away. First get married, then get pregnant, if she wasn't already, and hook him was the plan. If he left like her father did, at least she would get child support, alimony, or even the house so she could live off him and be away from her mother.

Chapter 2 - The Groom

Andrew, who was talking with the minister, watched the scene and realized what a mistake he had made inviting Juan to the wedding. He thought at the wedding there was a chance for a peaceful reconciliation but the look on Dolly's face told him that was not true. He could do nothing now but ignore the tension and explain it to Doreen later.

Andrew noticed his mother arriving with the "plus one" she insisted on her invitation. He didn't know that his mom was seeing anyone. He didn't like the idea of her being with someone. She always kept her private life secret from the family. Of course, he usually wasn't the least bit interested as long as he got the attention he needed and money to buy what he wanted. Could it be she was desperate enough to hire a date? He saw his mom walk away with her best friend, Brenda, to greet other guests and decided to capitalize on the opportunity to speak to the man alone. He decided to go over and pump this man for information.

"Hi," he greeted extending his hand, "I'm Andrew and you are?"

"David White," he replied.

"So how do you know my mom?"

David couldn't see any of Norma's features in the tall, manly looking adult that stood before him. The way Andrew walked suggested he had some military training. Well over 6-feet in height, the impression Andrew presented was one that would attract women. He wasn't necessarily good looking but roughly handsome. David gave a broad smile, more from nerves than pleasure, answering, "At the YMCA. I'm a professional dancer at the entertainment complex and teach on the side for fun and a little extra money. Your mom came to the class, but then her partner decided it wasn't for him. Your mom is very talented and it helps to have a good female to demonstrate the moves for the ladies, so I asked her to take on that position. We have become very good friends. While there is no time for competition dancing, we do go and glide across the floor regularly." Andrew did notice that in spite of having the over 50 look, David appeared to be in great shape. David was tall but shorter than Andrew, with a very slim build, white hair, and bright blue eyes. The entertainment complex David spoke of included restaurants, nightclubs, a movie theatre, and also included a stage show which Andrew assumed was David's place of work.

Andrew said, "I hope you didn't get fired after the computer malfunction the complex had, messing up the hours to work like Doreen did." David gave a questioning look. Andrew explained, "Doreen worked at the complex on a part-time basis because it was easy to schedule the work around her college activities. She decided to take off the week after the spring semester ended. When the computer went down, the company used the schedule from the year before. Doreen, having not signed up, didn't check to see if she was supposed to report to work and was fired for not showing up. She didn't find employment all summer even though she was out looking every day. She ran up a lot of debt on her credit cards, which we are still trying to pay. Surprisingly, she applied for a different job at the same complex this fall and got rehired. Those people are so stupid. They didn't know they had fired her."

David again gave him a curious look before a nervous laugh came out. "I'm not sure what you are talking about. Even though the limited position jobs like mine don't use the site, I never heard of the computer being down. The company policy is if the computer were to go down, they would use the schedule from the week before and contact each employee on the schedule by phone call. The turnover rate is so high that even many of the regular employees would no longer be there a year later, let alone seasonal staff."

"Did my mom ever ask you about the system?" Andrew wanted to know.

Feeling this was getting to be a touchy situation since Norma did ask and knew there was no computer breakdown, David avoided a situation by saying, "I don't know what Norma knows or doesn't know; you should ask her." David changed the subject by asking about the location and honeymoon plans. Andrew appeared to have a poker face with no reaction, except his eyes showed a flash of anger like there was a recognition that his wife-to-be lied to him. Andrew could also tell that David avoided the question, so Andrew assumed his mother did know of the deception.

Andrew suggested they go to the bar for a drink. David noticed Andrew had finished his third glass of champagne since his arrival but it was hard to guess how many he had before that. "Doreen likes this place because she felt like it was somewhere she would want to live. After growing up in a very small home with her mother, step-father and two sisters, she longs to be wealthy and have nice things. She felt she was born into the wrong life by mistake and deserved to be among the rich and famous. She never even tried to leave home and better herself. Twenty-six and Doreen is just finishing her Associate Degree. I guess that is why she wants me, to provide for her. I earn good money but still middle income, which is better than what she has."

Extremely taken back by the conversation, it was hard to hide the shock on David's face. "Aren't you in love?" he asked.

Andrew thought before he replied. "We are compatible in most ways. I'm getting close to middle age and haven't found the right woman. I figure I can teach her to be more mature and improve on her shortcomings. Her limited experiences in life have caused her to fall short of my expectations."

David had no clue how to respond to this confession. Norma didn't talk much about her older son. She didn't say anything bad about him, but it didn't appear they were close. He was beginning to understand why. Right then, a friend came up and started talking to Andrew so David used this opportunity to leave. He saw Norma standing alone and looking their way. David extended his hand, shaking Andrew's, before departing with, "It was so nice to meet you. If we don't get a chance to talk later, I do wish you the very best. Your mother is standing alone right now, so I should be a proper date and see if she needs anything to drink."

Chapter 3 - Norma's Family

"I can tell by the look on your face that you got a full dose of Andrew, correct?" Norma said with a hint of humor on her face.

"How can someone plan to get married with the intent of changing the person they are marrying to please them? That would never work," was the obvious statement from David.

Norma quietly laughed as she replied, "She intends to change him too. He just isn't smart enough to see it."

"Why didn't you talk to them, Norma? Words of wisdom are definitely needed in this case." David was worried that the look of sorrow on Norma's face was due to his harsh words, but a more troubled look in her eyes told him it wasn't.

Norma took his arm to walk where no one

would overhear them and said "Andrew has always ignored my words. In fact, he is very rude to me and yells at me if I say anything he doesn't like. I just keep my mouth shut, smile, and try to give him his way. I give enough to keep peace in the family." David could tell there was a lot more to the story than what could be told immediately. Perhaps Norma never told him because she needed to keep the relationship with her son to herself. He respected her privacy.

Changing the subject, Norma looked at the sky, and said "I sure hope it doesn't rain. Besides ruining the wedding, there isn't any grass under the first row where I sit and sticking my feet in mud will definitely mess up the timing of our dancing." The spark in her usually cheerful disposition returned quickly. He was glad.

There were a few guests present but it appeared there would be many more if the number of chairs he saw on the front lawn was any indication. A medical van pulled up with a car behind it. Norma made her way with a smile and a wave to the curb as David trailed along behind her. After hugs, Norma introduced David to her sister, Madelyn, and her husband, Mitch, and to her step-mother, Sandra, and her boyfriend, Daryl. Norma's son, Daniel, and her best friend, Brenda, came over to share in the hugs and greetings. David knew Norma's father died about six years before. After many years alone, Norma was glad Sandra had found someone that was good to her. Daryl provided good companionship and truly cared about Sandra. David admired that Norma was able to let go of the past and that Sandra's happiness was her first priority. Norma whispered to David, "I told Sandra that she was good-looking, kind and now very comfortable financially in life. So only keep a man around if he benefited your life."

Exiting from the van was Frank, a distinguished man in his early 80's. He was happy to see Norma and gave her a hug. Frank dated Norma's mother for 40 years and was like a father to her. Norma's mother was wheelchair-bound. This required the driver to open the wide doors in the back and position the lift to remove Betty from the van. Norma's face had a worried look as she viewed her mother. Frank and Norma stepped aside and whispered to each other. It appeared that Betty had suffered a mini-stroke since Norma's visit to the nursing home earlier that morning. They could tell by the way the right side of her face drooped and the way her mouth hung open in an unnatural way. Madelyn, Norma's sister, joined in the conversation. It appeared Betty's stroke occurred before Madelyn and Sandra went over to help Betty dress. Madelyn noticed something was wrong but didn't know exactly what it was. David thought

Sandra helping her deceased husband's first wife get dressed for the wedding was an unbelievable act of kindness.

The sky was overcast and getting darker; a wind was picking up. The temperature dropped to what felt like the low fifties, certainly not the best conditions for outdoor activities. The group moved quickly to an overhang that ran from the house to the old garage which acted as the bar. Norma grabbed a couple of blankets from her car and ran to cover her mother from the chill.

David entered into conversation with Sandra and Daryl by asking what they thought of the wedding. Sandra said, "We have not met the bride yet, so we have no opinion about the wedding or the marriage. I'm a little hurt to not have been introduced to the bride sooner, but I assume the couple did not have time to call or visit."

"You didn't meet at the rehearsal dinner yesterday?" David asked.

"The only time the facility was available for rehearsal was 11:00AM, so they had a luncheon instead of a rehearsal dinner. As out-of-town guests, we should have been included at the meal but the bride did not invite us. Instead, Norma had a dinner at her house last night for the out-of-town guests. Andrew showed up, but Doreen felt she had too much to do to come." Sandra refused to allow any slight rudeness to interfere with the joy at being at her grandson's wedding.

Madelyn and her husband, Mitch, went to the bar and grabbed hot drinks for everyone while Norma introduced her family to a few guests that were friends of Andrew. Norma's ex-husband and a girl half his age that hung on his arm like a prize stood away from the other guests and spoke to no one. The hateful looks given to Norma by the couple made David go over and put his arm around her as if to hide her from the negativity.

Chapter 4 - Doreen's Family Arrived

Multiple cars pulled into the parking lot at the same time. Car doors opened and Doreen's family all stepped out wearing black. Norma agreed with the sentiment that it was really a more appropriate color for the day. She had a lovely black velvet evening gown at home, but even though black was now an acceptable color to wear at a wedding, she still felt it was a little morbid. Doreen's family walked towards the breezeway laughing and ready to enjoy a good time.

Norma had seen some of the women at the bridal shower, but none made an effort to speak except one of the aunts by marriage. This aunt was also ignored during the shower except by Doreen and her two sisters. One of the uncles had recently divorced and remarried against the family's wishes, so Norma assumed that must have been her. Norma would have thought good manners would have prevailed and her future daughter-in-law would have introduced her to her family at the shower. However, good manners did appear to be one of Doreen's shortcomings. Maria made no effort to have a conversation with Norma either, but Norma felt that was okay because she figured that there would be limited contact between both of them in the future.

One uncle approached Norma and asked, "Do you know where we are supposed to go? Also, do you know where the registration book is?"

Norma responded, "I haven't been told anything myself. I haven't seen a registration book. There were no ushers or anyone with a plan on how the wedding was to transpire." Norma suggested, "Let's get a drink since the liquor has been flowing ever since I got here."

Norma, feeling a need to stay by her mother, was grateful when Brenda introduced herself to Doreen's family. Brenda guided the family around the building to where the service was to be held. The men, all of whom were in a playful mood, arranged the chairs in a circle singing the main theme to "The Lion King" titled "The Circle of Life." They only replaced the chairs back to the straight line position upon persuasion from Brenda. Then as more guests arrived, the uncles began to seat people themselves, trying to separate couples in order for more people to get acquainted. This playful humor ended up brightening everyone's mood, and soon people were talking and laughing even with strangers.

Someone pointed out that it was time to start, so everyone took their seats. Dave sat with Brenda in the third row on the right, while Madelyn and Mitch sat in the first row and were joined by Norma and her son, Daniel, when they marched in. The ex-husband and his child date entered the second row. The front row should have included Betty and Frank, but with the weather so bad and the wheelchair being too difficult to move on the grass, they took a position on the walkway. They stood where they would see the bride enter but not be in her path. The position was also surrounded by bushes to help block the 30-mile per hour wind from hitting Betty.

Everyone sat and waited quietly when an uncle joked, "At least, we are ready," getting a laugh.

Chapter 5 - The Wedding Begins

The wedding was being held at the front door of the old house. The house was made of red bricks, with its doors and windows trimmed in bright blue paint and a wheelchair ramp leading from the walkway to the front door. There were no flower beds or any decorations to soften the hard look of the building. It would have been so easy to add an inexpensive arch with flowers. Five dollars at the fabric store could have brought white cotton as a runway cover for the wheelchair ramp. It might have been a safety violation, but for the 10 or 15 minutes of the wedding, no one would have objected. Norma just shook her head at the lack of presentation.

The bride and groom both told Norma to keep her suggestions and opinions to herself. Her input was not wanted. Even though Norma wanted to be a part of the planning, she did as asked. Since she could have no say in the plans, she didn't offer to help with the cost of the wedding. She knew that the bride's parents paid about half the costs and that the remainder would be her son's bill to pay. Norma had a strong opinion that if you don't have any say, then you don't give any money, so that was ok with her. She gave $500.00 to cover the cost of the tuxedos for the groom and the two men standing with him, both of whom really couldn't afford the expense of the wedding. Her son informed her they were buying his preferred wedding attire instead of renting. It was always Andrew's dream to get married on the beach. Doreen refused to go along with the idea because she didn't like the beach or being near the ocean. Andrew and the men picked out white cotton slacks, blue blazers, white shirts and ascots with white, blue and red to match the girls' dresses. When Norma pointed out the inappropriate use of such causal clothes when the women dressed in more traditional clothes, her son yelled that he knew what he was doing, and her opinion was not welcomed. So the men looked like they were getting on board a dingy, while the woman looked ready for a yacht. Her money was not given with strings attached, so she figured they could use poor taste if they wanted. She had taken care of her son his whole life, and she wanted to make sure he had the funds to buy what he wanted to wear for the wedding, so she just responded with "whatever" after his tirade.

The door of the building opened and the men in the wedding party walked out. All of them had been drinking to a degree, but not by any means drunk. All of them had been sitting in their suits and now looked like they had been slept in. The only thing that looked right was that they all wore white canvas boat shoes so the whole outfit matched. The humor of the shoes was appreciated by everyone. Some of the men were secretly applauding Andrew's rebellion. After the men took their places, the women began their walk by leaving the side of the building and following the pathway to enter from the back of the crowd. Dolly looked a little nervous, but walked with good posture and nice even steps. Dolly's shawl draped carefully around her arms, per her sister and mother's instructions. Next, the youngest sister, Donna, was walking in but her gown didn't have a shawl. In fact, everyone hoped that nothing would fall out of the low cut top. The walk was more like slinking with her shoulders drooping. She was so much taller than her sisters that it was probably a habit to try to hide her height. Then the bridal march began. Doreen did have a lovely gown, one of good taste and probably a high cost, but on her head was something like an old-fashioned doily that people used on their chair arms. There was no front veil for the groom to lift, but maybe that was old-fashioned too. Norma noticed people were pointing to the back of the bride with smirks on their faces. When the bride moved into her position, Norma could see the wall of bobby pins holding up the back of her hair. The bride had two strings of hair in the front with the rest pulled tightly back and pinned with the metal so thick, it showed through the veil. Everyone guessed that maybe Donna was a little more jealous than she had pretended to be that her sister got married first.

The bride and groom tried to look lovingly at each other and appeared to be happy, but both were in fact angry with the other. Doreen's face practicing was paying off. She was so angry at Andrew for inviting her biological father without discussing it with her, causing her mother's irrational behavior on this day. Andrew was also practicing his poker face, being angry with Doreen's lie about being unemployed, causing them great financial difficulty. The red mark showing through the makeup on Doreen's cheek caught Andrew's eye. Even though angry about Doreen's deceit, he felt guilty about the pain he probably caused Doreen by inviting her father. He smiled, trying to assure Doreen that this was a new day and things would be better. It really didn't matter what the place or their clothing looked like, nor did it matter what people thought, this was their wedding and it's what they wanted that was important.

Today would totally change their lives forever. All that mattered was that the two were having their special day with a hope for a better tomorrow together.

The groom certainly didn't believe in church, preaching, or even God. He agreed to the preacher for the sake of the bride and her family. They went to church regularly and professed a strong faith in God. However, the bride couldn't stand the minister from her parent's church. She was required to only attend that specific church while living in her parent's home. They put out a call for anyone to locate a man of the cloth to marry them that would not require meetings or counseling. A retired Baptist minister agreed to do the service. Today was the first time he even saw them but didn't really care as long as he got paid. It was very clear that no sermon was to be included, so it was a quick service with the exchanging of vows that were greatly altered to be a limited commitment. Notably, the line "If someone objects to this wedding, let them speak now or forever hold their peace" was omitted, probably because everyone would have objected. Both had confided to their families all the dissatisfaction they had with each other, so the false pretense continued until they were pronounced man and wife.

The smile on Doreen and Andrew's faces as

they turned to face the crowd was picture perfect. Both had a look of joy as they marched past the guests. As the rows of people began their orderly exit, there was no reception line to greet them. No one knew where they should go or what was next on the agenda, so naturally everyone headed for the bar. Andrew and Doreen beat them there. Doreen was not a drinker, but appeared to be enjoying the vodka martinis. Andrew was always with a drink in hand when not working, but he seemed to be attacking the bottle with unusual zest.

Chapter 6 - Usual Photography Delay

Norma looked for her son to find out answers to all of the questions being asked by the guests, such as if they should be in the bar or in the main house. The staff was scurrying around her, moving tables from the outdoor patio where the reception was to occur to the three small rooms in the house. There was no rain, but the wind continued to whip and the temperature continued to fall.

The guests discovered their name cards with a table number telling them where to sit. There was no name card for Norma, David or Daniel. The lack of name cards for Norma and Daniel was clearly an obvious put down against them. Neither of them mattered to Andrew, except when he needed to have them do something to please him. Again, Norma and Daniel followed their usual logic of just smiling and getting through the day.

Andrew and Doreen had moved to the front door, standing at the end of the wheelchair ramp, taking pictures with Doreen's family. Andrew said he wanted to go ahead and take pictures with his mom and brother. Doreen, using the pouting face when she wanted to convey sadness that could easily be made happy with the right word, told him "Your family can wait until I'm done with my family." Andrew tried to dispute the point so Doreen stood for one picture, then said with irritation in her voice that they needed to get back to her family. Andrew told his mom to take his grandmother to the bar, so she would be out of the cold. They would do pictures later inside the bar area.

Forty-five minutes later, Andrew's family was getting tired of waiting. Norma went out and said something to Andrew about getting pictures. He and Doreen were drinking and talking with guests. "Not now," the surly Andrew replied. "We are still taking pictures here," which was obviously not true. About 10 minutes later, Norma asked the best man to intercede on their behalf. Again, the bride and groom refused to have pictures taken with Andrew's family. It was announced that everyone should go inside and be seated for dinner, and the director of the facility told Andrew that he needed to get the pictures taken with his family in order to not delay the serving of dinner, so Andrew and

Doreen walked into the bar.

One picture was taken of the family. Frank and Daryl stepped aside, since they announced the picture was of family and they were not technically a part of it. Then, one picture was taken of Sandra and Betty with the couple. No one understood why the ex-wife and widow would need to be in the same picture, but it happened. Doreen started to leave when Norma asked, "Couldn't we do one picture of the two of you with Frank and Betty and a second one with Sandra and Daryl?"

Doreen put her hands on her hips and in an angry low voice so her husband couldn't hear said, "One picture with your family is more than enough!" and marched out of the building.

Mitch, knowing the importance of treasuring the moment, decided to take pictures of the family as a whole and some of the individual couples, minus the bride and groom. Norma was faking her smile and showed outward composure, but inside was so angry. While the other family members went to locate their seats, Norma went into the bathroom and stared into the mirror, telling herself not to cry. The snobbish Doreen wasn't worth getting upset over. Her son would see the reality of what he married soon enough and while she wouldn't pay for the wedding, she would gladly fund the divorce. Norma was looking good with her hair and makeup perfect, so she put on a smile and walked out the door to face the rest of the evening. As she exited the bathroom, a slight quiver came to her lips, and she took a deep breath and shut the door very hard. She was proud she hadn't punched the bride. It was deserved, but this wasn't a hockey rink, and due to the selfishness of the bride, two-thirds of the guests were part of her family so it was best not to create a brawl.

"GET OVER HERE! GET OVER HERE THIS INSTANT!" bellowed Andrew.

Norma turned and saw her son with his hands on his hips, shouting so everyone could hear and realized he was talking to her. She quickly debated walking into the room to get surrounded by people, but it was obvious Andrew didn't care who was around, so they walked outside to try to get away so she could find out what was going on.

"DON'T START IT. DON'T START! YOU ALWAYS HAVE TO RUIN EVERYTHING."

Norma wanted to talk to Andrew, but it was clear that he wanted nothing but to shout at her and degrade her. She had no clue what was wrong or the reason for the attack. Andrew continued bellowing, screaming non-sense without even letting Norma speak.

"I'M THE MAN OF THE HOUSE NOW AND

YOU MUST OBEY EVERYTHING DOREEN AND I SAY TO YOU OR YOU'RE OUT OF MY LIFE! WE ARE THE BOSS NOW, YOU GOT THAT? UNLESS YOU LEARN YOUR PLACE, YOU WILL NEVER KNOW YOUR GRANDCHILDREN!"

The wedding guests were streaming out of the house to find out what the commotion was all about, then stood there staring in shock at the foul-mouthed, rude monster that Andrew had become. The best man, Russ, rushed out and tried to calm the groom but he couldn't get a word in edgewise either.

Finally with Russ in the middle of the two, Norma walked away. When Andrew stopped to take a breath, Norma quietly said, "You are out of the will," and with her head held high, walked away.

The always evil Maria was laughing so hard she could hardly stand. Norma said "This is your fault too, because you don't act human, and your daughters are just like you."

A Break From The Story

Priscilla's face showed her anger, "What a horrible young man. I can't believe he was so disrespectful not only to his mother but also to the wedding guests."

Belinda added her thoughts, "What a rude person the bride was. I think they deserved each other. She wondered why no one married her before, but a man would have to be desperate to enter into that family. How could any man with good sense be so blind to all that evil?"

Eve sat silent. She had made her share of bad judgment calls when it came to the men in her life, thus she didn't feel right giving her opinion on the bride and groom. Her only comment was, "It is so sad. I don't see how anything good can come out of this story."

Feeling the unhappy atmosphere of the ladies

on the porch, Josephine said, "I think we should stick to travel dialogue since the murder stories bring out such a sad feeling in people."

Eve pulled out her compact, opened it and started making faces into the mirror. "I don't even look in the mirror unless I have to. Do you think people really practice making faces?"

Jean turned and looked at Josephine.

Josephine's confession spilled out, "All right, I admit I was a face-maker in my teens but I certainly am not one now!"

Belinda added her own confession, "I use to practice my presentations in front of a mirror. It's a training tool so you can make sure if you are using proper posture, eye contact, and pointing to the screens correctly. I didn't do it out of vanity."

Priscilla pointed out, "No one is dead yet but there are certainly a couple of people I will cheer if they become the victim. In fact, I wouldn't blame anyone for getting rid of Maria, Doreen or Andrew. I certainly wouldn't want them in my life."

"Do you want me to continue the story or just forget it?" Jean was more than happy to leave some memories in the past.

"NO!" The word came out like a chorus from all the listeners.

Belinda said, "You have our curiosity up. You can't just let it go now."

Jean continued the story.

Chapter 7 - The Reception

Norma went inside to find Dave, Brenda, Madelyn, and Mitch talking at the far end of the house. "What's going on out there?" asked Mitch.

"Nothing," Norma replied with a smile. Dinner was being served but to obtain the food, due to the overcrowded room, the guests had to exit outside and go through the door of the next room of the building to get to the buffet. The return trip required holding the plates firmly with a second one on top as a lid to keep the 50 mile per hour wind gusts from blowing the food away. At least, it wasn't raining was the shared sentiment of the guests.

Norma was sick to her stomach after the attack and the thought of food was repulsive. While David and Norma had an agreement when dancing that they wouldn't drink, the bar felt like the only inviting place. Make-up artists know that drinking makes the foundation form clumping beads on your face, and dancers know your timing on the dance floor can get a fraction off, but Norma didn't care and went to get a glass of red wine. David understood how hard this was for Norma and stayed behind, pretending not to know where she was headed in case she would feel guilty for breaking their no-drinking rule.

Russ came out and got a glass as well. He hugged Norma and whispered, "It's not your fault. I think deep down, he knows what a mistake he is making and you have always been the person to absorb his anger." Norma relaxed her head on his shoulder and enjoyed the strength he provided.

Norma sat at the table watching the other family members, Betty, Frank, Sandra, Daryl, Madelyn, Mitch, David, Brenda and Daniel, enjoy their food. The photographer was taking the usual pictures of the various tables so the bride and groom could later see their guests enjoying the wedding. As the photographer was looking through the viewfinder to photograph the family, Maria came up and pushed the photographer to blur the shot. Maria loudly announced "We don't need any photos of this table and anyone around it." The family just sat there stunned, weighing the decision of whether to get up and tell this evil woman what they really thought of her and her daughter or act as mature adults should, knowing it wouldn't matter in the long run once the divorce came through. Mitch quietly got up, took the picture, and then sat down while the embarrassed photographer was being pulled away.

The cake was cut with the usual joking of whether to push the cake into the face of the bride, which Andrew didn't do, knowing he would pay for it at home if he did. It was Doreen's turn, and at first she didn't push the cake into his face, but ended up doing so at the end. Smiling at Andrew with her playful look, Doreen rubbed her hand down his face, adding tracks of food. The intent was to show who would be the boss of the marriage.

Russ had moved to the center of the room to do the toast, as required by the best man. He felt stuck in an awkward position, as he wanted to say "Let's call it a good party and go home" instead of congratulations. Russ began an unusual speech with praises of how his wife brought stability to his life and hoped the marriage would be a stable influence to Doreen and Andrew's lives. He refused to say any words without sincerity, so it was a short speech that focused on what marriage can be if both parties gave it their total effort.

"Can we talk?" Norma asked Brenda. With the guests returning to their seats, Brenda and Norma went out the front door and around to what was now the empty garage, formerly the bar. Norma explained what happened with Andrew. Always the compassionate friend, Brenda asked if Norma wanted to leave. Norma would've been totally justified in doing so, and Brenda was sure Daniel and David would agree.

Norma was about to leave when Russ's mother entered. "It's time for the Mother – Son dance." Norma looked at her bewildered, "I don't think that would be the best thing for either of us." The tender smile with the reassuring words that it would not only be alright, but something Norma would regret not doing in the future, convinced her to re-enter the house and sit at the family table.

Andrew came over and extended his arm. They walked onto the dance floor and began the simple swaying while stepping in a slow circle. Norma had tried to teach Andrew how to dance as a child, but it wasn't something he enjoyed. Andrew thanked her for showing kindness to her ex-husband and his girlfriend and making them feel welcome at the rehearsal lunch. Norma started repeating some of the funny parts of the conversations that had occurred when she visited with the couple. Her ex-husband said very little and was not happy about Norma and his date talking. Norma continued to tell any amusing story she could think of, and Andrew's laugh was genuine as he smiled at her. Norma noticed as they turned that Doreen pretended not to look at them, but was in reality looking constantly. The anger was easy to read but the perfectly acted faces still held their proper poses. As the dance ended, Norma said the words that were in her heart, "I truly do love you," but as he walked away, she knew she would never have a relationship with her son again.

Andrew and Norma's dance ended with the DJ saying, "That's the end of the planned dances. The floor is now open to all. Who will be the first to break the ice?" Norma just turned and extended her hand. David jumped up to take the hand with a smile and the two broke into an East Coast Swing.

From the crowds, they could hear comments like "They look like they could be on 'Dancing with the Stars.'" "What great moves!" "Yeah, way to go!" The other couples stayed off the floor but circled and clapped in time with the music. When the next song began, other couples took to the floor, but it was very obvious who the pros were of the evening.

The music selected had such a modern, fast-paced style that it eliminated Norma and David from performing their favorite dance, the waltz. Surprisingly, other than David and Norma, the dance floor was only occupied by a group of men from Doreen's family, taking turns doing fancy steps, and then standing back for the next man to try to top. These true gentlemen then went to every woman in the room asking them to dance, including cutting in to spend time dancing with Norma. David used the opportunity to include Brenda in the action. Brenda, who was not a dancer, tried to resist, but David assured her he would keep the steps simple and whisper instructions into her ear. The men then formed a circle dancing around Norma, and she had no inhibitions of dancing a solo. For Norma, it was a ruined night, but no one would know as Norma was determined to have fun and be the life of the party.

Guests began to leave, and as soon as it seemed tasteful to do so, Andrew's family headed to the door. Sandra, determined to do the proper thing, tried to congratulate the bride. Doreen tried to walk away like she didn't know Sandra intended to talk to her, but Sandra grabbed her arm. "We are leaving now, and I just wanted to express my best wishes and invite you to come to the house any time you are visiting with Andrew's father." Obviously, Sandra knew she was omitted from the last visit but was too kind to say anything or even take offense.

Chapter 8 - The Evening Ends

When Doreen went up to gather her things, she sat down in front of the vanity smiling. The evening couldn't have been more successful. She had planned the photography stunts, had no receiving line to avoid welcoming his friends and family, and had removed his family's seating cards to make them feel unwelcome. However, there was no way she could anticipate the horrible, degrading, tongue-lashing her husband would perform. The look of shock and hurt not only on her mother-in-law's face, but on the guests, was priceless. She hoped someone recorded that for her to view time and again.

There was another fresh martini on the table, probably a gift from her husband. She used to think Andrew liked to drink, but now she knows that he prefers to be totally intoxicated. Doreen lifted the glass into the air, trying to suppress her laughter so she wouldn't choke when she drank, and said "Cheers!" out loud, even though she was the only one in the room. She tossed back the drink entirely in one swallow, then made a face at the horrible taste. Doreen didn't like to drink, but that one tasted so bitter that had she not drank in such a quick motion, she would have spit it out. Doreen sat staring at the mirror, but she didn't know for how long. She could hear her husband laughing with some of his friends downstairs. She couldn't seem to move. The image in the mirror began to blur. The room began to spin. Doreen fell off the chair, landing like Sleeping Beauty into a deep sleep.

It had to have been about thirty minutes before Doreen was missed by Andrew and the remaining guests. The limo to take them to the hotel arrived. Andrew assumed Doreen was waiting upstairs to make her grand entrance. Andrew called up the stairs for her to come down. Knowing Doreen's flair for the dramatics, he assumed he was supposed to stand at the bottom in awe and sweep her off her feet. Andrew wouldn't be doing any sweeping because he knew he wasn't that stable on his feet. Truth was, he drank so much that he wasn't even sure he could perform that night but wanted to get to the hotel before he blacked out. Doreen didn't arrive as he assumed she would so he called up the stairs again. Perhaps, he wasn't thinking straight.

Maybe he was to escort her down, so he started up the stairs. By this time, the others in the room realized something was not right and gathered at the bottom of the steps. Andrew walked into the room and saw his wife on the floor. He called out her name while rushing to her side. Doreen was not responding and was out cold. He noticed the empty glass on the floor and figured it was just one too many. After all, she was a lightweight when it came to drinking. Maria ran into the room ranting, "You stupid girl, ruining your wedding with the evil of alcohol! I told you I didn't want liquor at the wedding," she shouted at Andrew. Maria tried to kick at the girl, screaming, "Get up, you have to do a proper exit!" Andrew caught Maria's leg, jerking it upward to keep the foot from landing on the unconscious girl, sending Maria sprawling on the floor. All the commotion caused the remaining guests and family to run up the stairs into the room to see Maria with her dress around her waist looking like a fool. This added to Maria's fury.

Andrew said "I think we should take Doreen to the hospital."

"She is breathing, just drunk!" Maria screamed. "Don't you dare take her to the hospital to add to her shame! Besides, she doesn't have insurance and until you file the marriage license and make her officially your wife, you don't have the right to sign for her. If I sign the paperwork, the hospital might come after me for the money. Take her to the hotel. She will be fine in the morning."

The limo driver could hear the shouting and decided to break the rules and leave the limo to see if he could help. Andrew was trying to help Doreen to her feet and encouraging her to stand. It was obvious the groom was in no condition to carry his wife, so the driver offered to help. "Are you sure she's ok? Maybe we should go to the hospital?"

"NO! NO! NO!" shouted Maria, so they went to the car.

As they drove to the hotel, while alone with the groom he again asks, "She doesn't look too good to me. Now that we are away from that horrible woman, that offer to go to hospital still stands."

Andrew was really too far gone to use good judgment and knowing that the hospital would call Maria and another scene would occur, decided on the hotel instead. "I think she just had a little too much to drink and will be fine in the morning."

At the hotel, the driver helped by carrying Doreen to the room. "In all my years of driving, I never carried the bride over the threshold before." Andrew gave him a good tip, then shut and locked the door. By the time he got to the bed, his head was spinning as he fell in next to Doreen, both still in their wedding attire.

Andrew woke up about noon the next day. His head was so hung over, he couldn't figure out where he was. He turned and saw Doreen was still in her dress. "We are man and wife," he said while stroking her face. Doreen didn't respond. Andrew went into a panic. His heart was racing as he called Doreen's name and gently moved her arms and shoulders. With no response, he lifted her eyelid and noticed that her pupils were dilated and her breathing was labored. He grabbed the phone and pressed 0 for the operator. "My wife, something is wrong! Call 911!"

A Break From The Story

"I'm tired of talking right now. Do you ladies want to join me for a cup of tea at Fannie's?" Jean asked. Fannie's real name was Francesca Ann, but she decided years ago she preferred to be called Fannie Annie. She and Jean became best friends when they were in their early 20's and were very dedicated to each other as true best friends. Fannie and Jean used to travel together a portion of each year, but when Jean decided to come off the road permanently, Fannie couldn't stand the boredom of the Friend's Home. Jean had a routine of getting up about 10 AM, a small breakfast, stories on the porch, tea in the early afternoon followed by water aerobics, dinner, and then writing until late into the night. Fannie decided to open a second hand store called Fannie Annie's Attic, which is located two blocks down Fourth Street, then one block south on Main St. from the Home. Jean had lobbied for a tea shop in order for the friends to have a place to gather each afternoon. Fannie hated tea, but Jean decided to keep tea at the store over her objections. Fannie's days were taken up with working at the shop, either taking in consignments or attending rummage sales and auctions in the larger towns and farms to obtain merchandise. All the ladies were willing to sit at the store while Fannie did her trips.

"We're here for our tea," said Jean as she entered the shop.

Fannie shot her a dirty look. "I don't have nor sell tea." This exchange of words was another part of the routine. Jean kept cups and tea at the shop and made it for herself and anyone with her on these afternoon visits. Fannie continued their routine. "You are going to get me in trouble someday with having tea and food here." Fannie turned to the other ladies in the room, "Do you agree that Jean is so stubborn?"

Jean gave her normal response, "Well, technically, I am serving the tea and no one is paying for anything, so no one is selling it."

Josephine looked at the table on display near the register. "Isn't this Molly Frisk's table?"

Fannie looked up trying to decide whether to share the gossip or not. "Molly sold her house and decided to move to Forest City to the new senior high-rise that is so luxurious. She is moving soon, so I went over yesterday and brought a lot of the items over here to sell for her. I don't think it would fit in your little rooms at the Home but it would look nice in your dining room, Belinda."

"It is nice, but I have a family heirloom that I don't want to part with in there," said Belinda.

"I can't believe she sold that house." said Eve. "She has lived in that house since birth."

"Too big and too hard to take care of," explained Fannie. "She is in her 80's and it takes a lot of work and money to keep up the house. With no one to help her or any descendant to leave it to, she decided to accept a sizable offer and live more comfortably."

Jean left for the bakery next door. When she was out of ear shot, Priscilla couldn't wait to ask, "We are hearing a story about a bride drinking a spiked martini at her wedding. The story also has a drunk, obnoxious groom. Is that a true story?"

Fannie might tell about the house sale but she would never reveal something Jean might not want known. "I'm not sure what story you're talking about."

Priscilla, not getting the hint pressed on, "There was a wedding at the church and when they left and the car horns honked, Jean acted weird. I keep asking why she didn't like weddings until she told the story. We are at the point when the bride is being taken to the hospital after being such a wicked person at her own wedding."

To evade answering Priscilla's question, Fannie asked, "Does the lead character have a best friend in the story?"

Priscilla brightened, "Yes, named Brenda. Is that you?"

Jean walked back in just then, and Fannie, being the colorful person she is, didn't like her role being labeled Brenda. "Really?" she said looking over the top of her reading glasses. "Brenda? What a boring name!"

While the ladies enjoyed their tea and snack, customers walked into the store. "Come join us!" Jean invited. "Isn't this a lovely table to sit at for tea? It's a very old family antique from one of the town's founding families." Fannie shot Jean a look indicating she should handle the conversation from there. Indeed, the couple did have tea and did leave after purchasing the table.

"It's time to walk home and get ready for our water workout." Eve noticed. "Is the story going to continue there?"

Jean smiled knowing that Eve didn't like to work out as often as she should and that the story would be the only thing to get her to exercise. The slight smile that crossed her lips was not lost on the others. "Yes," she replied, "It will be three parts. Part two will be this afternoon and we'll finish tomorrow at our normal story time."

"Ok, I'm coming," said Eve without enthusiasm in her voice.

Chapter 9 - The Hospital

Andrew let go of Doreen's hand just long enough to go wash his face. He had been crying almost non-stop for a week. His eyes were red and swollen. He returned to his seat, giving Doreen a kiss on the forehead as he sat down and took her hand again. Doreen was in a coma and had not responded since they entered the hospital. Andrew tried not to start crying again as he thought about that dreadful day. How could everything he and Doreen planned gone so wrong? He should be the king of the world today, returning from his honeymoon and boss of his domain. Andrew started thinking back over the past week.

When they arrived at the hospital, Doreen was rushed immediately back into a room with a team of doctors and nurses working on her. Andrew went to the desk and tried to do the admitting paperwork.

When asked about Doreen's insurance, he didn't know the answer. Emily, the admitting personnel, was trying to help him since Andrew was beside himself with grief and his head really wasn't totally clear from the night before. Andrew told Emily about the wedding when she looked at him with sorrow and had to deliver yet another blow. While the intent was there for them to be husband and wife, until the marriage certificate was filed, Doreen wasn't on Andrew's insurance and he couldn't legally sign any of the paperwork. With no other options, Andrew provided Maria's phone number to the staff. Emily called to tell Maria that her daughter had been admitted and she would need to come right away to help with the paperwork.

Maria arrived in her usual over-the-top, loud, obnoxious attitude. She was crying for her perfect daughter and telling everyone what a loser she married. Maria finally realized the seriousness of the situation; her daughter was in a coma and probably would not live. Maria started screaming at Andrew, blaming him for her daughter's condition. What did he do to her wonderful girl; had she drank more after the reception; did he give her any medication? Maria ran at him and started pounding on his chest, yelling "WHAT DID YOU DO? WHAT DID YOU DO, YOU HORRIBLE MAN?" Her shouting was so hostile that Emily called security, who took them into a back office to try to work out the story. Maria blamed Andrew for Doreen's condition.

"Throw me under the bus, you bitch? I'll get you!" Andrew admitted he was so drunk that he couldn't use good judgment but told them how Maria tried to kick the helpless Doreen and refused to let him bring Doreen to the hospital. He could remember the limo driver making the same suggestion to Maria, who stood firm that Doreen was not to be taken in for medical help.

The security officer said if there was any further yelling or discussion of the situation, he would throw them both out.

Maria begged to see Doreen, but the medical team was still working on her. Maria and her family were taken to one waiting room and Andrew was taken to another. They were assured that Doreen's progress would be reported to both rooms, and if either went to the other's waiting room, that person would be kicked out.

Andrew learned later that Maria refused to sign the paperwork for Doreen because she might have to pay for it. She told the staff to let the medical bills pile up and let Andrew pay them off. The hospital was required to continue the care for Doreen because it was not permitted for a hospital to refuse a person in a life-or-death situation.

Andrew called his father the minute he was alone and begged his dad to come to the hospital and be with him. His father refused to come.

"I needed to catch my plane and return to work tomorrow. You understand, don't you, son?"

Andrew didn't understand and felt like he was being deserted once again. The man never stood by his side through a problem nor would he ever loan him a dime. Andrew had his father on a pedestal and did everything requested by him, and now when he needed his father the most, he was told no. Andrew remembered how he degraded his mother. Norma was always by his side and supported him emotionally and financially, but his father and Doreen told him how proud they were when he yelled at Norma and how much she deserved it. Norma was the most patient person he knew, but she had her point of no return, and he knew he crossed it at the wedding.

Instead of Norma learning that she had to obey him, she walked off saying, "I really do love you but you are out of the will." That, in Norma's terms, meant he was out of her life. If he called and apologized, she would probably come be by his side, but this would disappoint Doreen if she ever came to. Doreen wanted Norma to be second place on everything. It would also make his father respect him less to cave into his mother's caring arms.

Andrew decided he would have to be a man and tough it out alone. Russ had been a good friend for years and was someone Andrew could call for support. Russ and his mother both came to be with Andrew in his time of trouble.

Andrew's friend, Barbara, was already scheduled to look after his pets so he called and told her the situation. Barbara told him that she would take care of the pets and his house, so he wouldn't have to worry about returning. She also agreed to sit with Andrew if Russ had to leave. What a great friend. Andrew dated Barbara a few years ago, but they found they were better friends than lovers. Andrew was so glad she was still in his life.

The hospital staff permitted Andrew and the family to see Doreen when she was finally in intensive care hooked to life support machines. The tension was heavy in the room, but it appeared that Doreen's step-father had talked sense into Maria.

Visitation times were agreed to by both parties. Maria would come up after work and stay until eleven at night, but for the rest of the time Andrew could be there. It actually worked out good because it would give Andrew time to go home to shower and eat. He didn't like leaving Doreen alone, and even though it was intensive care, the staff agreed to let him sit quietly with Doreen.

He talked to her in a soft voice in case she

could hear him. Andrew reviewed all the plans they made for the future. He poured out his heart to Doreen about his love and grief. He apologized for being too drunk to understand the danger she was in. Andrew recited poems and even created his own heartfelt poems about her. At other times, he just sat quietly, but he thought maybe Doreen could feel his presence. He wanted her to know that she wasn't alone.

Andrew called his work to let them know what had happened, even though he was on vacation. His boss came to the hospital to offer his support. When Andrew explained about Maria not signing the hospital admittance papers, his boss advised Andrew not to file the marriage license. The liability of the medical expenses would become Andrew's if he did file the paperwork to make them man and wife. Since Doreen was already in the hospital, even if Andrew added her to his insurance, since this would count as a preexisting condition, the insurance would not cover any of the medical expenses, which was over one hundred thousand dollars by now. Andrew liked his boss's suggestion to look like a true romantic by saying that the marriage license would be filed when Andrew and Doreen could walk into the courthouse together.

It had been a week and still no brain waves were evident. It was decided to remove the life support, hoping she could continue to live on her own. If Doreen could breathe and her heart continued to beat on its own, then a feeding tube would be inserted. If not, then they had to accept that it was her time. Andrew felt fear and dreaded this day. He hated that he was all alone at this difficult time. His father talked to him on the phone a couple of times a day, but refused to return. How Andrew wanted his mother's love and support, but he refused to call her. She would know what to do and would not be afraid to put Maria in her place. She would have defended Andrew through any situation, but Doreen and his father were so proud of him for belittling Norma. If Doreen didn't die and woke up, she would be very upset that Andrew called his mother. He had no choice but to face this alone.

The hospital scheduled two policemen to be there when the family was ushered in. The machines were turned off and Doreen passed into whatever world is after this one. Maria and her family prayed, but Andrew didn't believe in God and stood quietly with tears running down his face again.

After a few minutes, Maria marched over to the police officer and insisted that he arrest Andrew for the murder of her daughter. She then ran towards Andrew to hit him, but the officer was quicker than

Maria. The policeman called over the radio to the station house for instructions and it was decided that the police detective would speak first to the doctors and then go to each of their homes for the interviews. Maria was livid, but her husband managed to pull her away and they left. The officer that stopped Maria's attack suggested to Andrew not to take any calls from Maria and if she came to Andrew's house, he should call the police immediately and stay inside with the doors locked until they arrived.

Andrew gathered his and Doreen's personal items to leave, but realized he was too upset to drive. The chapel was open so Andrew went in, not because he believed but because it was quiet and he could think. He was sobbing loudly when the hospital priest came in and sat next to him. The understanding man didn't say a word but just sat with his hand on Andrew's back and handed him tissues as needed. After an hour or so, Andrew got up to leave. The priest asked if there was anyone to call to help with the drive home, and Andrew shook his head regretfully and walked out the door.

Chapter 10 - The Investigation Begins

Detective James Murphy and his partner, Detective Jessica Johnson, were assigned the case with a warning that the mother of the deceased did not seem to be mentally balanced. The best place to start was with the doctors that treated Doreen, so they sat in the office at the hospital getting any information the staff could provide about the case. Dr. Jacobs was well versed in the information the detectives needed, so he suggested he would give a statement and then opted for questions at the end to clear any matters he might have omitted.

"Doreen was admitted on Sunday around 12:30 pm. She was in a comatose state brought on by a combination of drugs and alcohol. She never came out of the coma, and by the end of Sunday there was no brain activity on the monitors. The type of drugs was unknown. The husband and family never knew

Doreen to use any drugs at all, and drinking was very limited. There were no medical signs of any prior drug use, and no signs that the drugs were forced on Doreen in any way. Doreen was about three or four weeks pregnant, so she probably didn't even know about the baby. She appeared to be healthy and in good condition when the lethal dose was given."

The hospital administration liaison told of the fighting that occurred at the hospital and their involvement in being fair to both the family and the groom in visiting with Doreen. The hospital provided statements by employees that had conversation with either of the two parties to help with the investigation. The time and place of the wedding was given to the hospital in order to help with the treatment of the patient by providing the length of time the induced state occurred as well as information on the food intake. The hospital refused to offer any other opinion on the family, except to disclose what they witnessed themselves and the steps taken to keep the hospital peaceful and fair to all concerned.

Hoping to obtain more facts before the interview with the family, and armed with the name of the venue where the wedding took place, the detective's next step was to interview the employees that represented the facility during the event. The venue hostess, Helen, proved to be very helpful. She detailed the entire wedding from her point of view. The family was disorganized, and she felt she had to step out of her normal responsibilities for the wedding to not be a complete disaster. There was no one to hand out the flowers to the right people. No one was available to assist in the seating of the guests. There was no information about where the guests should go or the flow of the events. Helen was very surprised the groom was still standing by the time the wedding began, considering the bartender reported Andrew finished an entire bottle of champagne by himself. Details of the lack of interaction with the bride's immediate family, the mother, father and sisters as well as Doreen, with the guests, including their own relatives, did not escape the watchful eye of the wedding planner. Pictures were taken with the groom's family only after she approached him and told him the food was being served, and either the picture needed to be taken now or would have to wait until after the meal. She had the feeling neither the bride nor the groom wanted to act civil to his family even though she had no clue why. Helen didn't understand the logic of inviting someone when they clearly didn't want them to be a part of the day. She witnessed the degrading attack by the groom on his mother but again had no details as to why it occurred. Helen did see the bride drink a few drinks that were Vodka Martinis. The groom requested a pitcher be available for her benefit. The wedding was already the worst in the history of the facility, and that was before the final disaster at the end when the bride collapsed. She described in detail the interaction with the mother of the bride and the groom when they found Doreen's body. Helen thought Andrew was too drunk to know what was happening but he at least realized they should have left for the hospital. She was amused when the groom placed the mother on her bottom when Maria tried to kick the poor bride. It was Maria's insistence that Doreen was not to receive medical attention. Helen said she disagreed with the decision but didn't feel she had the authority to overrule the mother.

James asked Helen about her impressions of the family on previous meetings before the wedding. "I felt the bride and her family were very snooty. They acted like the world should bow down to them. I really had a bad feeling about them and hoped they wouldn't choose this as the wedding location, but I'm here to make the sale and had no reason to turn down the business. I only hope there won't be any bad publicity over this our lovely location." Helen was obviously worried about her job if word got out it was the house of death. Helen continued by showing them the invoice, which revealed the payment was made by the groom. "Until the wedding day itself, I thought Andrew was ok. He wasn't stuck-up or rude like the others, but when the bride was out of the room, he was a little too flirtatious for my taste."

Helen provided the name of the limo service and the name of the driver. She recommended the company often when helping customers with their wedding plans. The detectives continued to their next stop.

The limo driver was Adam Smith. Few people asked his name or opinion on anything, so he was surprised when the police came to interview him. He was polite to customers and kept to himself, which was the best way to earn big tips. As drunk as Andrew had been, he did give Adam a good tip after he carried the bride down the stairs and into the car. "What a total joke that family was." Adam detailed the time of his arrival, his going into the house after the yelling started. "You won't tell the boss I left the limo, will you? I could get fired for that, but I did lock it up and keep it safe."

Detective Murphy assured Adam nothing he said would be repeated unless it was absolutely necessary. "I assure you, Adam, you did the right thing through the whole event, and the police have no desire to get you into trouble, so please continue."

That made Adam feel very relieved. "I felt

guilty about not taking the bride to the hospital. I could tell her condition was more serious than the others thought. I made the offer twice. The first time was when the wild woman went after the groom and when I made the suggestion, then the wild woman turned on me, too. The second time I suggested the hospital was to the groom alone in the limo. He did understand that if we went to the hospital, they would call the looney woman and it would be hell to pay all over again. He declined my offer, so I did what I was told." He laughed at the unusual circumstance about him having to carry the bride over the threshold, and then helping the groom as well.

Detective Johnson restated the assurance that Adam did the right thing because she could tell how bad he felt when he learned of Doreen's death.

Chapter 11 - The Dreaded Wild Woman

Murphy and Johnson were being paged on the radio by Violet, a very smart but firm woman that controlled the reception desk at the police station. "You need to return to the station NOW! Maria is here to talk to you with her two daughters in tow. She's yelling that the police are ignoring her daughter's murder. I told her you were on the way and would like to talk to her in the conference room. That's where I put her for now, so hurry before she comes back out."

Murphy responded, "Thank you for handling the situation. We will be right there. We are only 5 minutes away."

He turned to his partner, "How do you want to handle this? She seems to hate men and yet craves their attention at the same time. You might get more out of her with the 'we are women in this together' attitude. I also have a worry that if I don't appear to believe her, it will be 'all men are alike and cover for each other'."

Jessica laughed, "Aren't you being a bit of a coward?"

James in defense said, "No, if you want, I will enter the den of the dragon lady, but someone needs to interview the two sisters. They might not open up to you because you are a woman of power and authority." Even if he really didn't want to interview Maria, he would have done so since it was his job.

Luckily, Jessica relented to James' good reasoning. "You're right, I will let you know if I don't click with her and we can swap." Detective Johnson was always very serious about her job and did not use humor about work.

"Good thing you are here," said Violet. "If that witch comes out here again, I might be the next one being investigated for murder."

Johnson smiled as she said, "It sounds like you would get off for justifiable homicide."

Murphy and Johnson entered the interview room, introduced themselves, and then Jessica took the lead. "Maria, I think it might be better for us to talk alone. It would be more confidential and less upsetting to your daughters. I suggest Detective Murphy go get them a drink from the break room, and then they will be in the next room if you want or need them. We have coffee, tea, or soft drinks available."

The three exited, leaving Detective Johnson a chance to slip into the seat across from Maria at the table. "I'm so sorry for your loss, Maria. Is it ok for me to use your first name? You can call me Jessica if you like."

Maria felt that Jessica was a kindred spirit and warmed to her instantly. "I waited at home like the police at the hospital told me, but I didn't hear from you. I thought maybe you didn't care."

Jessica used a soft, low voice while shaking her head sadly, "Of course I care, but I felt I needed the facts before approaching you for questioning. I interviewed the doctor and others to make sure I understood the situation. You appear to have accused your son-in-law of something very serious and I would like to hear why you think he was involved. I will let you tell the story your way. I will save any questions until I hear your story in full, and then ask questions at that time, if that is ok with you."

Maria liked the patronizing manner as well as feeling in control of what was being said, but she couldn't control the tears that came and went. Her grief of losing her daughter was very real.

"I don't consider him my son-in-law. He didn't file the marriage license. Trying to get out of paying the medical bills, I bet. He did pay for most of the wedding, which his part was about $10,000.00. He offered to help pay for the funeral, so I might let him come if he does come up with the money.

Andrew is a very foulmouthed, heavy-drinking man. He thought he controlled Doreen, and she let him think so but planned to change that after they married. She was afraid if she exerted her authority too soon, it might scare him away. He makes good money, so she planned to get pregnant immediately, and let him know who was boss. If he didn't like it, at least she could get enough child support to live a good life without working too much. I didn't know she was with child until we were at the hospital. My heart is so broken over losing not only my daughter, but a grandchild too.

Doreen would never do drugs, so I'm sure the drug and drink combination that killed her was not self-induced. No one in my family would ever hurt someone. We are a close family and love each other very much.

Andrew didn't appear to like his family at all, especially his mother. With our large family, there was only room for him to invite 25 people. His father was as drunk as Andrew was and could barely stand. Doreen was introduced to the father and a girlfriend over a long weekend visit last summer. She liked him okay and the girl wasn't even the same one. The father lives far away and so into his own life, she didn't really seem too concerned about his interference in the marriage. Andrew appeared to care more for his father than the father cared for Andrew. The dad and a woman were there but didn't interact with anyone else. Doreen had limited contact with Andrew's side of the family except for one meeting with his Aunt that she got along with her okay. Andrew's grandmother is very ill and could not have gone up the steps to the room in which Doreen died, so I don't suspect her. Besides, Doreen and Betty liked each other.

I hate the mother, Norma. She thinks she is so much better than anyone else. She didn't say so but she made no effort to be nice. I invited her to dinner. She came and never returned the invitation. Is that bad manners or what?

Dolly asked Norma if she was excited about the wedding, and Norma said she didn't care if they got married or not. She said she would accept what her son wanted to do about marriage. She was so lucky to get such a perfect daughter-in-law like Doreen, and she was so uninterested in the wedding. She told Doreen that every woman should plan to contribute to the family income, and you never know when you might end up raising a child alone, so she should finish her education and get work experience before having children. I take it she was planning on taking her son away from Doreen as soon as she could and relieve him from his responsibilities to support his family. I think she was jealous of the relationship, like Doreen was stealing her son.

Another reason I think it could be Norma is while I don't like her, she is not a stupid person. I taught my daughters to control the relationship with a man in any way possible. Doreen liked to use sex. If there was a plan to be with Andrew's family, Doreen would be so overcome with desire to have sex at about the time they should leave. She would tell Andrew his family would still be there, and suggest having sex before they leave. Norma was upset because they would arrive to meals late, and the dinner would be ruined.

There were times when Andrew was supposed to help take his grandmother to the doctor or help transport her to a different nursing home, and Norma had to get help from someone else at the last minute because Andrew didn't show up. He was in bed with Doreen. Norma had the nerve to tell them that if they promised to do something, that they should do it on time, and that to show up late was rude and disrespectful. Andrew never fell for the sex delay again.

Doreen, being so clever, knew Andrew's desire to shop, so she started using the technique of suggesting to Andrew that they stop to get him something. Anything would do, such as a new shirt, to look at new door handles for the kitchen, to shop for the centerpieces for the wedding. Andrew considered buying something for himself to be more important than being with his family. Norma got so mad but didn't say anything. She just quit asking them to come over to her house. Norma would tell them about family events but not wait for them to arrive before serving a meal or opening presents. If Andrew and Doreen suggested getting together, she would remind them to be on time.

I was so happy when, for some unknown reason, Andrew went ballistic on Norma at the wedding. I don't know what made him mad, or what he was yelling about, but he was so ugly and mean. It was a dream come true that their relationship had ended without it being something caused by Doreen. That's why she might be the murderer. If Andrew didn't do it, it had to be Norma. No one else had a reason." Maria started sobbing, "My little girl was so wonderful. We were very close, and she was emulating me. She would seek my advice, and we planned the dating, wedding and the future step-by-step together. She would control Andrew and still be my loving, attentive daughter obeying me.

The only other person was my ex-husband, Juan. It appears he was invited to the wedding, and Doreen was as shocked as I was to see him. It had to be Andrew who invited Juan. I had Dolly tell him to leave immediately and he did. Juan is a terrible person, so maybe he was so mad at being told to leave, he came back to kill his daughter to hurt me. Do you think that a man would do that? Men are such beasts, they need to be controlled.

Jessica, you look so surprised. Did your mother not teach you how to control men? No wonder you are single, you poor child. If you like, I would be glad to talk to you when you are in a relationship and give you the years of my wisdom and advice."

Chapter 12 - Are There Any Facts?

The stunned Detective could only shake her head, "I assure you my mother didn't teach me the same things you taught your daughters. I appreciate the offer for help, but right now I'm not in a relationship. If I ever am, I assure you that I'll remember your words." Jessica made the sentence sound diplomatic, but her true thoughts were to never apply Maria's bad advice.

Maria smiled very pleased with herself.

Jessica had a lot of questions, so she began, "If you thought the relationship was going to be so bad between Doreen and Norma or that Norma would try to break up the marriage, why didn't you suggest to Doreen to wait and consider if it was really the best action?"

Maria was confident in her response, "You must not know how to handle children, Jessica.

Doreen was in her mid-twenties and very old not to be married. It was embarrassing for her and for me. Andrew could have been trained to know his place, as long as he didn't have the support of his mother. So, instead of trying to get Norma to like Doreen, it would be better for all concerned to get Norma out of the picture. With no one to support him, it would have been easy to get Andrew under Doreen's thumb."

Jessica managed to keep a sincere look on her face and not show how repulsed she was by this woman. "Do you have any clue why Andrew, who just married Doreen, would want to kill her? Isn't getting married an act of love, not a step to get rid of someone?"

Maria looked a little guilty, "At my suggestion, Doreen told Andrew a lie that she was fired from her job this summer. Andrew totally believed Doreen was unable to find work all summer when in reality she didn't even try. Doreen needed to teach Andrew that they could live on his salary and she didn't need to work. Norma brought a man to the wedding who told Andrew the truth. I don't know if Andrew really believed the man, but it did bring doubt. Also, Andrew was very firm that he didn't want children until Doreen got her degree and worked. I didn't know if Andrew knew about the baby or not. Maybe he didn't want the child so much that he would kill them both. He may have considered the deceptions a reason to kill Doreen. All I know is she was ok when she left the wedding. Maybe a little drunk and couldn't walk on her own, but I would bet he got the pills and stuffed them down her throat later."

Jessica was angry at the comment that Doreen was ok when leaving the wedding. She was glad they talked to the limo driver and got the truth of not only Doreen's condition, but the rudeness of Maria trying to kick her helpless daughter. "You didn't think Doreen should go to the hospital at the end of the wedding? You thought she was ok?"

"Of course," said Maria, "She was drunk but fine otherwise. I would never have let him take her away if I thought my daughter needed me."

"Let's go back to the wedding venue, did you see anyone go upstairs around the time the wedding ended?" Jessica was trying to get some facts, not just loose and unfounded statements.

"No, I didn't," replied Maria.

"Did you see Norma go upstairs at any time during the entire event?"

"No, she avoided the women in the family, I think. Norma certainly shook her back side with all my brothers. She was on the dance floor until she left."

"What time did she leave?" finally getting somewhere thought Jessica.

"Norma, David, Daniel, Brenda, and the entire family left about 9:00. The wedding was scheduled to last another hour. Andrew's father and the bimbo left about ten minutes later. He was drunk, and his girlfriend was mad at him and was attempting to get him out the door for a while, but I think he was holding his ground until Norma left. All the people that were invited by Andrew left within the 9 to 9:30 time frame. You would think they would have stayed to see the couple off."

"Please describe the room at the time you realized Doreen needed help. Can you tell me who was still there, and finally, who might have gone upstairs in the final hour?"

Maria thought before answering, "My husband and I and all three daughters, Andrew, the best man, and two other men that served in the wedding, some of my brothers, sisters, and their spouses were there at the end of wedding. Andrew wouldn't leave early because he said he paid so much for the party that he planned to enjoy every minute of it. The Wedding Coordinator, some men taking down tables, and a couple of people in the kitchen packaging up food were there from the venue. The limo driver came in after we found Doreen to help her down the stairs. As to your second question, there was an empty martini glass on the floor, a few clothes lying around the room that Doreen was getting together, plus her sister's and my things were there. The makeup previously on the dressing table was lying on the floor. That's all I can remember."

Jessica, feeling like things were going nowhere, acted a little tougher, "Maria, I believe your claim that Doreen didn't use drugs, but we have no evidence to work with. The house was totally scrubbed clean, the empty dishes and glasses removed, and no witness to anything. You didn't see anyone upstairs and can't give me any particular action or reason to suspect anyone except three people you don't like. I need something here. Please think hard and tell me if you can remember anything."

Maria's face got a look of understanding. "I'm sure both of my daughters and I saw Andrew go upstairs just before it happened."

The smug look made the lie even more irritating. "I think we are done here." Jessica stood up, leaned forward, resting her weight on her knuckles on the table. "You can't live life on a lie."

Maria, totally shocked at Detective Johnson's anger, retorted, "It's not a lie if you believe it. I believe Andrew killed my daughter, so I'm justified in anything I say."

Detective Johnson told Maria to stay in the interview room until her daughters returned, and then they would be escorted to their car.

Chapter 13 - Dolly's Interview

James left the interview room with Dolly and Donna to go to the break room. Donna preferred the green tea while Dolly opted for the coffee. As they walked past Violet at the reception desk, James asked Donna to have a seat so she would be with an officer. James instructed Dolly to follow him to a different interview room. Dolly froze in her tracks, wanting to know why they would go to an interview room and why Donna wouldn't be with them.

"Do you believe Doreen's death was self-induced?" James asked.

Dolly shook her head no.

"You want to help find out what happened to your sister, don't you? People often don't realize they have important facts to contribute to the investigation. We will just be talking so I can get a better idea of what happened."

Dolly, clearly uncomfortable with the idea of talking, asked, "Did you get our mother's permission for the interview?" James assured her that she was an adult, and he didn't need her mother's approval.

Donna stepped forward and placed her hand on Dolly's arm, "It will be fine. We have to do all we can to help."

Still fearful, Dolly suggested, "Maybe it would be better for us to all talk together."

Trying to sound patient and reassuring, James said, "People remember things differently, even in the same situation. If you say something, Donna might think she remembers something incorrectly. Too many people hurt the flow of a conversation. I will talk to Donna after we talk, while Detective Johnson is speaking to your mother."

Dolly sat perched on the edge of the chair like she was ready to run. James smiled, "Relax. Remember, I'm the good guy here." Dolly tried to fake a smile, but one wouldn't appear. James started, "I'm really sorry for your loss. Were you and Doreen close?"

Tears were shining in Dolly's eyes as she replied, "She was my best friend. We did everything together for years. I miss her so much and can't believe this is happening."

James kept his voice soft and quiet, "You said you don't believe Doreen took the medication intentionally to hurt herself, but could she have taken something just to relax her nerves before the wedding?"

Dolly answered by shaking her head no.

"Do you know of anyone that wished Doreen harm?"

Again, Dolly shook her head no.

"Did you see anyone go upstairs before Doreen went up to gather her things?"

Dolly repeated her gesture of no.

James took a different approach to try to get a conversation going, "Why don't you tell me everything you can remember about the wedding day. Start with what time you arrived, what was the mood of each person, tell me about Andrew and his mother, and tell me anything you want to say, even if you consider it unimportant."

Dolly didn't want to talk but with Detective Murphy just sitting in silence staring at her, she knew she had no other choice. "I'm afraid to talk because if I say the wrong thing, Mom will be mad at me."

James now understood the fear was not of him but of repercussions from Maria. "I promise no one will know what you say to me. That is another reason why I wanted to talk with you alone. It's really important to hear everything we can about that day for your sister's sake, so please trust me, this will never get back to your mother."

Dolly thought about what to say. She knew some things would make Maria mad, like talking about her mother hitting Doreen before the wedding or trying to kick her when she was down. Dolly would keep it simple and not say anything negative about anyone. "I loved my sister very much and was proud to stand with her as the bride's maid. She let us pick our own style of dress so we, Donna and I, could feel more comfortable in front of the crowd. Everyone was in such a good mood. Doreen was especially bright and cheerful. The only negative thing was our father arriving unexpectedly. All of us were shocked since it was fifteen years ago since we last saw him. Mom, Doreen, Donna and I thought it best for him not to be there, so I went and asked him to leave. Juan, I won't call him father since he hasn't been one to me, didn't seem upset at all. Juan turned to Andrew, thanked him for the invitation but never thought it would work, got in his car and left. Everyone was relieved to see him go, and we went back to the perfectly planned wedding.

The only other event was Andrew going

ballistic on his mother. There didn't appear to be a reason, and we were all surprised. Norma just walked away as her son was screaming. I wouldn't have blamed her if she left, but she stayed and tried to have fun. She avoided Andrew and Doreen the rest of the night. She left as soon as she felt she could, about 9 or 9:30. Other than those two things, the wedding was beautiful and perfectly normal, of course until the end." Dolly's voice was normal for a little while but became quiet and filled with sorrow at the end.

James could tell Dolly had no intention of being totally honest so he decided to get more specific. "Do you like Andrew? Was the groom in a good mood? Do you think that Andrew was drinking too much?"

The slight smile on Dolly's face was genuine, "Andrew always drinks too much. He was in a good mood, bad mood and back to good a couple of times during the wedding. Andrew is known to have mood swings, and I figured the pressure of the wedding didn't help."

James jumped in to ask, "Do you like Andrew? Do you think he could hurt Doreen?"

Dolly paused to give herself time to think of the right answer, "I don't think Andrew could ever hurt Doreen or anyone else physically. I like him as Doreen's boyfriend, not mine. I wouldn't want to put up with his belittling manner. It didn't show up when they first started dating but surfaced later. Doreen could ignore his rudeness. She would say there was good and bad in everyone, and what she couldn't tolerate, she would later change when she took control. Doreen would say that Andrew just needed a good woman to love."

"What is your opinion of Norma, Andrew's mother?" James didn't know if this was important but it would keep Dolly talking.

"I like her. She was nice to me and would ask me questions, like my thoughts were important in the couple of meetings we had. I had to keep the conversation short because Mom and Doreen were watching, and they didn't like her. I don't think she liked Doreen, but I didn't get the impression she disliked her either. Norma said she was ok with whatever her son wanted."

James disliked the next question but felt the need to ask, "Did you know Doreen was pregnant, and do you think Andrew knew?" Dolly could only shake her head no and the tears began to flow, so the interview was done.

Chapter 14 – Donna

James walked Dolly to the seat next to Violet, who shot him an irritated look as she handed a tissue to Dolly. Donna patted Dolly's shoulder as she got up and walked to the interview room without James saying a word.

"Thank you for the interview. I am sorry for your loss. I want you to know that anything you say will be kept in confidence." Donna rolled her eyes and looked bored. The differences between the sisters' personalities were great even though they had similar features in their faces. Donna was taller, slender, and confident to the point of arrogance. Dolly was fearful and had no confidence at all, shorter and a little heavier than the rest of the family.

Donna bluntly responded, "I don't say anything that I can't say in front of everyone. I take it from your introduction to the conversation that Dolly was afraid of saying something that would get her in trouble. Dolly always tries to say the right thing and wants to please everyone. Dolly needs to learn what other people think doesn't matter, and that you can't please some people ever."

This opened a whole new avenue for James to explore. "Do you mean your mother or someone else?"

Donna realized she had said too much, so tried to make light of it, "Mom especially. The more Dolly tries to make her happy, the more she says negative things to Dolly. Mom isn't happy unless she is stepping on someone's feelings. I just tell Mom what she wants to hear and sneak behind her back and do and say what I want."

James tried not to smile as he asked, "How did your mother get along with Doreen?"

Donna, reverting back to the bored attitude, said, "Doreen was smart like I am. We play Mom the same way. Another big difference is that Doreen and I have confidence and planned our escape; Doreen by her marriage to Andrew, and I am getting engaged soon, so I have my out. Dolly makes enough money to leave but is too afraid to fail and have Mom throw it up in her face. I don't see what any of this has to do with Doreen's death. We might have personality challenges, but we are a family that loves each other and sticks together."

James realized this line of questioning was over, so he went the more traditional route. "Do you think Doreen overdosed by accident and if not, do you know anyone that might want to do her harm?"

"No to both. Everyone liked Doreen, and she would never do drugs."

James observed Donna would look around the room like she was alone until she thought he said something dumb, then she would stare at him.

"Did you see anyone go upstairs near the end of the reception? Why don't you tell me in your own words the events of the day?"

Donna again looked at him like he had three heads, "Nothing you probably don't already know. It was a nice wedding and everyone had a good time. One ugly incident when Andrew went into a screaming fit at his mother but nothing else big."

James thought it was really odd to leave out the part about seeing her father for the first time in fifteen years, so he asked her about it. Donna looked as if she didn't care, "I was two when he left fifteen years ago. I don't know the man, and he isn't my father. I really don't consider his being there anything big except the rudeness of it all. The man must have some ego to think he would be wanted or welcomed. No, I didn't see anything unusual, and I saw no one go upstairs after we came down about 9:00."

James was surprised, "You went upstairs when the reception was going on?"

Donna snickered, "My boyfriend and I thought it would be funny to, you know, like the mile high club, but we call it a wedding club. You know, find somewhere at a wedding to do it before the bride and groom even has a chance."

James' jaw dropped at the thought that there was a wedding club. Was he getting old or was the girl just unique in her view of what was acceptable? He asked, "Was the martini glass in the room at that time?"

Donna realized the importance of the question but had to disappoint him with her answer, "The bride's room was closer to the stairs so we went into the room that the groom and his friends used which was at the end of the hall. I didn't look into the bedroom where it happened so I don't know."

James continued, "What time did you go up? You said you came down at 9:00, right?"

Donna really wanted to help but couldn't. "We went up at about 8:45. It was only a quickie because of the risk of getting caught. I didn't see anything, or I would tell you."

James tried the next line of questions that he used on Dolly, "Can you think of anyone that would do Doreen harm, like an old boyfriend or someone else in the family?"

Donna was ready with her reply, "I have done nothing but try to think or remember. This is my sister, and I truly cared about her. I just can't think of anything."

"Your mother accused Andrew of the deed at the hospital a few times. What is your opinion of Andrew and his family?"

Donna blushed. "Mom was a real asshole at the hospital. I wanted to hide. I wouldn't date Andrew myself, but Doreen seemed happy enough. Andrew drinks a lot and has a big mouth. I don't think Andrew did it, but I do believe that if he wasn't so drunk, he would have seen the danger Doreen was in and got her help. I don't know his family at all. I only saw his mother twice, at the shower and at the wedding rehearsal, and never spoke to her. She was on Mom and Doreen's shunned list and I had no reason to go against their wishes."

James shouldn't have asked the next question, but did anyway, "You said if Andrew wasn't so drunk? Couldn't the rest of the family, yourself included, see Doreen was in bad shape?"

Donna's temper showed but not at James.

Donna was mad at herself. "I have questioned myself every day about that. I thought she should go to the hospital but decided it wasn't my place to say. I will never make that mistake again. I'm not a doctor, but I knew Doreen was in very bad shape. I just wish I would have opened my mouth and said it."

A Break from the Story

Belinda looked sad and was shaking her head no. "I can't believe anyone is as cruel as Maria. I wish it had been her to die, not her daughter. I wonder if she ever realized how miserable she made her own children."

Priscilla stated, "I would have been out of there the day I turned 18."

Eve again was the thoughtful one, "The girls just didn't know what life could be like. Usually, mentally abused people never understand they have the right to change their lives. They often end up marrying someone like their parents. I don't think she would have had that much better of a life with Andrew."

"I like the Detective Johnson character," said Jean. "I can relate to her spunk."

Josephine laughed as she said, "Oh, I thought you would relate better to James. I think the bad weather at the wedding was an omen."

Priscilla broke one of the rules by insisting on an answer, "Is this story real? Is there really someone as wicked as Maria?"

Josephine responded, "Yes. There really are people that are that cruel and unloving."

"Speaking of bad weather, we need to hurry and finish our workout before that cloud moves our way." Jean, leading the aerobics, handed out noodles to the ladies and ordered, "Let's get to our core work. Put the noodles behind our backs and pull the knees to the chest for 100 crunches. We will get 500 stomach exercises in the next 5 minutes. Let's keep exercising while I finish the story."

Chapter 15 - Notes to Compare

With the family escorted to their car by a uniformed officer, James thought to himself about how boring real investigation work could be. James dreaded this case. Not only were there no clues, but being a big event like a wedding meant he would listen for hours to the same story over and over again. Being real detectives, he and Jessica would ask the general questions in a polite manner, and then listen intently to the answer, looking for that obscure statement or inconsistent fact that can lead you to the truth. He often wished his job was like the hour detective shows where you asked questions in a gruff voice and the people broke down and confessed. What made this case even worse is that the participants have such a distorted conception of reality, it makes it harder for him to ascertain the facts.

Ready to compare notes with his partner, James went to the desk area where Jessica was already sitting. Jessica kept a supply of rubber balls of different sizes in a jar on her desk to squeeze to build arm and hand strength. As he sat, James causally made the statement, "That is one messed up family."

Jessica erupted in an unusually loud voice, "That's the understatement of the year. If those girls were minors, I would call children's services to get them taken away."

James realized that he needed to give Jessica his full attention. He should have realized that tossing the ball from one hand to the other was a sign that she was really concentrating on some thought. The bad thing is not only did he come to that realization of how angry Jessica was but so did the detectives working in the area who all turned to look at them.

Various comments started to come from people around the room, "Did you throw you partner into the lion's den, James?"

"Why didn't you man up, James, and take on the wild woman yourself?

"Brad is getting married. Learn any lessons on how to control a man from the mom?"

The last comment caused the ball to leave

Jessica's hand and go across the aisle to hit the detective who said it. Right then, the chief came out of his office, picked up the ball, and handed it to Jessica, "Just like the softball game we lost against the firefighters. The ball just slipped from your hand again?"

James reacted in time as Jessica rose and turned to throw the ball at the chief's head as he walked away. James caught the ball and put it in the bowl. Taking Jessica by the arm, James said, "Let me get you a cup of coffee."

Jessica, not to be out done, responded, "You always buy at the office where it's free."

The two detectives took their cups and went to the picnic table outside the office. There was little privacy at their desks. "Ok, let's hear about what has you so fired up."

Jessica had trouble sitting still and started to pace. "That woman either thinks I want her to lie so we can arrest Andrew, or at the very least, she thinks if she lies, I will let her get away with it. What kind of person does she think I am? I told her the truth that with no witnesses and no evidence, there wasn't much we could do. She wanted me to go arrest Andrew right then with no proof. I know now she will tell people in her family to lie, and if they are anything like her, we have a problem."

James tried to lighten the mood by saying, "If there are more like her, the world has a problem." He got the laugh he hoped for from Jessica. They compared notes on what each woman said. The photographer was a friend of Andrew's, so the next course of action was to interview the photographer where they could get that information and hopefully see the crime scene in pictures. It had been a long day already, but both detectives were single with not even a pet to worry about, so they decided to continue working into the evening. They also needed Juan's address from Andrew and planned to talk to him the next day.

"Why do you think the girls put up with the mental abuse by the mother?" Jessica was a very strong, independent woman and would never tolerate that kind of family life.

"They just don't know any difference. They don't know how a normal family should function," answered James.

Jessica then got the laugh from James when she announced, "When I get home tonight, I'm calling my mother and telling her what a wonderful job she did raising me. Really, I don't thank her enough, but that will change."

James was sincere when he apologized for not interviewing Maria himself, but Jessica assured him they made the right call. "Either she would have been fake to get you to flirt with her, or she wouldn't have talked as much because you are a man and not to be trusted. It doesn't get us anywhere, but at least I feel she exposed her true self to me. Andrew doesn't know how fortunate he is not to get into that family. I'm sure right now he can't see it, but it would have been a nightmare."

Chapter 16 - Andrew's Interview

When the two detectives knocked on the door, they were greeted by a very sleepy and confused Andrew who invited them in. The room of the ranch-style house in a large subdivision was a mess with eight empty beer bottles on the table.

"I was sleeping. I haven't slept any all week except sitting up at the hospital. I only came home from 6:00 to 10:00 each night when Maria was there. I would come home and shower, change clothes, grab a bite to eat when I could stomach food, and then went right back to the hospital. I kept thinking that if Doreen woke up, I didn't want her to be alone. You're not here to arrest me, are you? Do I need an attorney present?"

James took the lead on the questioning, "You haven't done anything to be arrested for, did you? You are permitted to have an attorney if you like, but I honestly don't know if we even have a case."

Andrew still appeared confused. "The way that bitch Maria went on, I thought you might believe her garbage. I'm suffering so much, and that bitch keeps yelling so all the hospital can hear that I killed her little girl. Maria doesn't drink, and yet she didn't see Doreen needed help. I wanted to take her to the hospital, and Maria wouldn't hear of it. If anyone killed Doreen, it was Maria with her lack of action."

Jessica didn't really want another cup of coffee, but thought it might do Andrew some good. "If you don't mind, I would like to go make a cup of coffee. When was the last time you ate?"

Andrew thought, "I don't remember when I ate for sure. I can make the coffee if you like."

Jessica was already in the kitchen and shouted, "If I can't find something, I will let you know, but I'm good."

James offered, "If you don't feel up to this, we can come back later. Are you alone? Is there someone you can call to stay with you?"

"My best buddy, Russ, came over when I arrived home from the hospital after the plug was pulled. I was too upset to drive, so I hung around the hospital for about an hour. I called him when I left, and he was here when I arrived. We sat and had a couple of beers, but I must have fallen asleep. I had a cover on when I heard you at the door so Russ must have covered me up and left."

Jessica returned from the kitchen with coffee and an egg sandwich. Damn thought Andrew, Doreen couldn't even cook, and here this girl is not only nice looking, must be smart to be a detective, she can cook and even shows consideration. I need to keep her in mind after this all passes. Andrew looked Jessica up and down, then looked in her eyes as he delivered a sincere thank you for the food. "Doreen never cooked before. I taught her to cook coffee and eggs. I thought if I looked up slow enough, maybe it would be her." Andrew really wasn't flirting or cheating on Doreen in his mind. He always had a way of turning on the charm around women even if he didn't like them. He was glad to see they accepted his explanation.

While Andrew was eating, James got the contact information about the photographer and the guests that Andrew invited to the party. He was only permitted to invite around twenty friends and family members, so the list was short.

James noticed Andrew looked a little better after the sandwich. "Do you know what happened to Doreen? Do you think it could be an accidental overdose, or do you think it might be more sinister?"

"I've never known Doreen to take anything stronger than an over-the-counter headache medicine. She always complained of headaches. Doreen liked to be in control of her thinking and didn't drink much, so I can't imagine her taking a strong drug. I know I don't have any pills or medicines at the house and wouldn't have given it to her even if she asked. She did spend the night at her mom's so we wouldn't see each other the night before the wedding. I don't know if they have anything there."

James was interested in the next question even if it was a repeat, "If you think it was drugs, who do you think would have given them to her? I suppose you know Maria accused you, your mother, Norma, and her ex-husband, Juan. Do you think they would do it?"

Andrew was very mad at this point, "Mom would never do harm to someone. She would walk away and leave them, but never would she use violence. Juan was long gone and never saw Doreen. I saw him come, and never took my eyes off him until he left, so it couldn't be him. Why don't you look at that bitch causing all the noise? Maria is an obsessive control freak especially with her daughters. I know she acted ok about the wedding, but I think she was upset at losing control over Doreen. I've made it very clear that I didn't want Maria controlling our lives and planned to move out of state as soon as Doreen finished her degree. I don't know anyone else that would do Doreen harm, but the big hand print on the side of Doreen's face when we exchanged our vows proved Maria didn't mind harming Doreen. I don't remember much but when Doreen was lying on the floor passed out, Maria tried to kick her. That I remember, and I was glad I put her on her ass."

The new twist created a new question for James. "A hand print on her face? Do you know who put it there and why?"

"Hell yes, I do," said Andrew. "When I saw Doreen's face after she came down the aisle, I wanted to know then but she mouthed 'later' so no one would see. We went to the bar after the ceremony, and Doreen said Maria hit her because of Juan being invited to the wedding. Doreen was really mad at me for inviting Juan and made it very clear she was unhappy about it too. She didn't want to see her father again. My mistake, I thought because she talked about him now and again, even though he had been gone fifteen years, that she had a desire to see him. I now know that it was a warning to me to avoid making the mistakes that she felt Juan made with the family. I was supposed to be learning what to do and not do. Trying to mend the fence was not what I was supposed to do.

That's why I invited him, and I'm sorry I did. Dolly came down and asked him to leave, but she did it really nice and polite. I'm sure Maria sent Dolly because I saw her watching from the window."

James continued, "What about your mother, Norma? I understand there was quite the scene with her. Would she have taken it out on Doreen? Did she like Doreen?"

Andrew clearly didn't want to talk about his mother but there was no way out of it. "Norma would never hurt a soul. Even if she disliked someone, she would walk away and not talk to them. I don't think Mom liked or disliked Doreen but was willing to be nice and accept her since I wanted to marry her. I think I can say with certainty that Mom would never give pills to Doreen."

Clearly, Andrew was avoiding the scene he caused with Norma but James felt it might be important so he pushed the question. "What was the scene about? You don't think it has anything to do with the case?"

"No it doesn't. Ok, here it is. I have a love-hate relationship with my mom. She always provided for me and stood by my side emotionally and financially, but I hate her because she took me from my father at a young age, about the time I was two years old. It's bad enough she deprived me of a father but at the age of thirty, she decided she wanted another child. I was all she needed in life; she didn't need to have another child. My dad always told me how selfish Mom was and pointed out when he felt her decisions didn't benefit my life. I would tell Dad when Mom made me unhappy or I didn't get my way, and my father told me my mom was wrong to treat me that way. I wanted to live with him, but he said that Mom needed me. If she needed me and I was to be the man of the house, why didn't she listen to me or give me my way? Dad told me I was the man of the house, and the man is the boss, so she wasn't giving me the respect I deserved. I dreamed my whole life of telling my mom off. A few years ago, I was supposed to be marrying Kim and I told my mom as soon as Kim and I married, I would never see or speak to her again. I planned the same thing with Doreen by my side. I would kick my Mom out unless she obeyed me at all times. I didn't mean to do it at the wedding, but she was clearly upset over something. I have no clue what was wrong, and it made me mad that she would be upset on my wedding day. I didn't ask questions. I just started yelling at her. I guess all those years of hate just spilled out. She walked away like she always did. I thought she would leave the wedding, but I think Russ and his mom worked to keep her there and calm me down. Usually, after one of my degrading tongue lashings, we don't talk for a while until I go and act nice. I never apologize, but usually she will take me back without talking about the incident. I will admit she is the one that stands beside me, and I could have used her support at the hospital. Doreen and Dad both went on and on about how proud they were of me for putting her in her place. If I call Mom now, I would be betraying Doreen and disappointing Dad. Besides, even Mom has her breaking points, and I doubt if she would come unless I said I was sorry for yelling at her. And I won't do that because I'm not sorry at all."

Both detectives were very shocked at such an attitude but tried to hide it. Jessica decided she could get more information with her understanding way. "Did your Mom mistreat you, beat you, or wrong you?"

Andrew looked indifferent, "No, not at all."

"So if your father wants your Mom out of your life, why didn't he stay to help you through this?"

Andrew was again clearly upset, "Good question, but I have no answer. I talked to him before he left and begged him to come with me to the hospital, but he said he had to get back for work. We talk daily and he finally agreed to fly back down after we knew that the plug would be pulled so he could be here to support me at the funeral. I know he isn't rich but he gives plenty of time and money to the girl of the month. I don't want his money, just someone to stand by me."

Andrew was fighting the tears now. He felt so very alone. "Dolly and Donna both came to the hospital during the day when their mother wasn't around. Dolly was especially nice and supportive of me. Donna didn't act mad or mean, but I know they both fear Maria. That's why I wanted to get Doreen away. I kept telling Doreen we would have a family in a few years so I could rid myself of my mom and she could be away from her mom."

There was a shocked look on Jessica's face, "You didn't know?"

"What?" asked Andrew.

"Doreen was pregnant."

Andrew started sobbing and shaking his head no. After about fifteen minutes, he could barely speak, "No, I didn't know. I thought I didn't want children yet, but to know I lost one…" Andrew started sobbing really hard again so the detectives were afraid to leave.

Andrew finally called Russ, who came over. Russ assured the detectives he would stay as long as necessary.

Chapter 17 – Juan

Jessica tried not to start the interview with any preconceived ideas or opinions about Juan but she didn't like the fact that the man hadn't seen his daughters for fifteen years. Jessica expressed her opinion to James about Juan's lack of character, but was reminded not to judge before they had the facts. Why wasn't this man fighting to protect his girls?

Juan was surprised when he opened the door to the detectives and let them in. The house was clean and bright with pretty colors and patterns on all the furniture and walls. Many would say a little overdone, but Jessica liked the cheerfulness. Juan's wife was in the kitchen getting tea and returned to sit next to her husband. "Can you please tell me what this is about?"

It was apparent Juan didn't know about Doreen. Upon hearing the bad news, the man cried and kept saying, "My poor baby!"

Jessica couldn't help but ask, "Why did you leave your daughters? Why didn't you see them?"

Juan was shaking but able to talk. "My ex-wife was a vicious and vindictive woman to me, but she did seem to love the girls. She got mad and threw things at me all the time. One night, she came at me with a knife for no good reason. I arrived from work late, but she didn't believe that I was working. I never cheated on her. I did volunteer to work overtime a lot because I hated to come home to her and because she didn't work, so we needed the money. I had to grab her wrists to keep from getting stabbed so it caused a bruise on her arm. She called the police and I got arrested. There was no one to witness that she pulled a knife but the evidence of the bruises supported the story she told of me being a wife beater. She wanted a divorce and made a deal with me that if I went away and left the girls forever that she would not press charges of assault. Maria said her sister and one brother agreed to testify that they saw her bruised up a lot, and with the bruises the cops saw, I knew they would win. I didn't want to leave my daughters, but I hoped with my being gone, Maria would be a nicer person. Besides, what good could I do for my girls if I was in jail? Maria had a restraining order against me, and if I had a criminal record, I couldn't get a job to support them. I took the deal and left, even though I was devastated to lose my daughters. I found happiness with my new wife, and we have a lovely home and family. I am truly happy, even though I felt less a man for leaving Dolly, Doreen, and Donna.

My wife didn't think it would work for me to go to the wedding, but I had to try. She was totally supportive and understood it would make peace for me. She also was understanding and supportive when I came home rejected. I left as soon as Dolly asked me to. I could tell she didn't hate me, so at least that made me feel better. Please tell me what happened to Doreen. Are my other two girls okay?"

James and Jessica looked at each other because they both felt the girls were not 'okay,' but they were not permitted to render an opinion. Had Juan knew the situation of his remaining daughters, he would have been in more sorrow than he already felt. James approached the subject carefully, "We don't know if Doreen took pills and then drank not realizing the combination would harm her, or if someone slipped pills into her drink. We have uncovered no prior evidence of drug use. We can find no one that disliked Doreen. We know Doreen lived at home, that is until she moved in with Andrew. We really don't have any more information than that right now. I'm so sorry to have to deliver the bad news. I know it's been a long time since you last saw her, but do you have anything you can add?"

Juan said, "No, I wish I knew something about my daughter's life but I don't."

James continued, "Needless to say, we have to ask what you did after you left the wedding."

Juan was calmed down by his loving wife's hand touching his hand. "I drove straight back. I left at four and got here about 7:30. My wife can verify the time I left and returned. I stopped for gas on the way back and paid for it by credit card." He got up and got a receipt from a box. "We put all receipts here until we compare them to the bill that arrives each month but if you need it, you can have it."

Juan's wife got up and put the receipt in the printer and scanned a copy. "Here, this way we both have a copy. I don't trust Maria. She will blame Juan if she can, so I think it is best to keep proof that Juan returned directly home in case detectives, besides yourselves, come to call." Smart woman thought both James and Jessica.

Jessica broke a rule of not getting too personal when she asked, "Why did you marry Maria? Couldn't you see she wasn't a very nice person?"

Juan smiled and asked his wife if she wanted to be there when he gave the answer. She said yes, and Juan began, "Men often think with the wrong head.

Maria showed up at the fast-food restaurant I worked at one day and fell in love with me. She wanted sex a couple of times a day. Being seventeen and not too bright, I obliged her. Maria assured me that she was on the pill and wouldn't get pregnant. It was a month after I was eighteen when she announced she was with child. I didn't want to marry her, but back then it was the right thing to do. My parents said I had to take responsibility for my actions, so I married her when she was about seven months along. I put all of my efforts into making the marriage work, but it takes two for a successful marriage. Maria kept getting pregnant so I told her I was getting fixed. She said she would have the surgery instead so I couldn't cheat on her. I think the reason she would let me go without paying child support was that she had someone else that could provide for her better than I could, but I never tried to find out. To be honest, after the nightmare years together, I was so thankful to be free."

As they walked to the door, Juan had one last request, "If you ever get the chance, please let Dolly and Donna know I'm here for them. This month was fifteen years since I left. I looked it up in the Statutes of Limitation, and Maria couldn't have me arrested after that long. It was so good to see Dolly."

As the detectives got in the car, they saw Juan

and his wife holding each other close. They were glad Juan did find happiness and Jessica admitted, "I stand corrected on my opinion of Juan."

Chapter 18 - The Crime Scene

The photographer, Willie Mayor, was home from work. Photography was a side job that he hoped would become full-time. James and Jessica dropped by this home/studio and were reviewing the photos from the wedding. "Why aren't there any pictures of Andrew's family except the two in the bar? I can see in the photo of the room they are seated in the far corner. Doesn't the photographer take a picture of each table? Why do you have shots of the other tables and no close up of this one?"

Willie didn't like discussing his clients because if word got out he talked about his customers, it might be bad for business. "The people that hire me deserve their privacy. I took the shots as the customer requested. Pointing out I didn't do a complete job might scare off potential clients."

James looked up with a serious frown and said,

"One of your clients is dead. That might hurt business, too."

"Alright, Maria, the mom and Doreen made it clear not to take pictures of Andrew's friends and family. They said after that night, they would be in his past and the pictures would be a negative reminder. I tried to take a picture once, only to be pulled away by Maria like a bad child. It was embarrassing getting scolded in front of everyone as she reminded me again of her instructions. The wedding was normal except the picture request, the yelling bout with Andrew at his mother, and what I would later realize was the murder scene. I felt really bad for Andrew's mother. I don't remember her name but I know she was really upset."

"Norma is Andrew's mother," reminded James.

"Andrew and Doreen kept them waiting for an hour before they went in and took the two pictures. After one group shot and one with the two grandmothers, Doreen turned to leave. Norma asked if Doreen and Andrew would have a picture taken with the grandmothers and their boyfriends separately. It appears one was the grandmother, one was the step-grandmother, and it would have been nice to have a picture in which they didn't both appear together. Doreen refused and pushed Norma aside to walk out. I thought Norma was going to cry and saw her go into the bathroom. When she came out, Andrew started yelling without asking what was wrong or giving her a chance to speak. He said things like, 'You will obey my every wish or never know your grandchildren.' I have never seen such an unkind act. I felt sorry for Norma because I didn't see her do anything wrong to be talked to so rudely by the bride and the groom. Norma just walked away and Maria was laughing so hard I thought she was going to fall over. Norma looked at her and said, 'Your daughter doesn't know how to act like a human being and neither do you. Hope you are happy to have Andrew in your life.' Maria was surprised and before she could respond, Norma was walking off. Maria had an angrier than usual look on her face and went in the other direction.

I made copies for you of the guest tables and the shots around the venue from about an hour before Doreen was found. Most of the guests had gone home and I took so many shots earlier that I held off from taking more until it was time for Doreen to come down the stairs. The last batch is the room and pictures of Doreen. There's Doreen lying on the floor with an empty glass beside her. Those items, like make-up and hair brush, were on the dressing table as you can see in this before the wedding photo. Doreen probably knocked them on the floor as she fell. There is my favorite, Maria on the floor after Andrew pulled her leg up to keep her from kicking Doreen. What a bitch that woman is.

Have you had a chance to talk to her much?"

James answered yes but the look on Jessica's face told it all.

James was looking closely at the wedding shots, "Did you notice if there was a handprint on Doreen's face?"

"Yeah, now that you mention it." Willie pulled out a few photos, "Here is one when the ladies were getting ready and as you can see, no handprint. This is when the bride marched in and if you enlarge this area on the cheek, you can see red. There is a lot of makeup though, so it would be hard to prove if it was a handprint or not. It looks like a hand to me but I didn't notice it until you said something."

James and Jessica left with the usual, "Here is my card, call if you remember anything." There was a sincere thank you for the photos, which they took back to the office to study.

Chapter 19 - Dead Ends

The next day the detectives visited with everyone on the guest list, but there was no one that added any information. One of Maria's sisters and one of her brothers both said they saw Andrew go upstairs at approximately the right time to leave a spiked drink, but they happened to be the two that were willing to testify against Juan, so there was no credibility. Naturally, Doreen's family claimed she was a wonderful girl, and most even liked Andrew, so it was a total waste of time.

Phone calls were made to the various out-of-town guests, all of whom were members of Andrew's family, to see if they could help on the timing and placement of people. Those that were interviewed had left the wedding before the incident with the bride. Andrew's family really didn't know Doreen at all and they didn't believe Andrew would do bodily harm to anyone. None appeared to have known about Doreen's death prior to the phone call from the police. The detectives thought it was curious that Andrew hadn't informed his family about what had occurred.

James and Jessica consolidated their list of facts, suspects and clues and came to the realization they had nothing. Maria thought it was Andrew, Norma, or Juan. Juan had proof he was in the clear. Besides, both detectives liked Juan and didn't feel he would hurt anyone on purpose. Andrew thought Maria did it to get the attention and not lose control of her daughter. Knowing the life of this woman made the detectives think there could be some truth to the accusation, but again there was no proof. No one else appeared to have a motive to even be a suspect. Doreen had only dated once before for any length of time, and the boy walked away saying she acted too much like her mother. That was about eighteen months before she dated Andrew. He was at Miami University and didn't even know or care about the fact that Doreen was getting married. All the detective could do is keep asking questions, hoping someone would mention some fact they didn't realize was important, but with no crime scene, there was little hope of proof.

Jessica was holding her head in her hands when she said her true thought, "Most of these people just are not nice. In fact, I would say some of them are mentally messed up." It's usually better to interview the unbiased people before getting to the suspects, but in this case it wouldn't have helped. No one had said anything of importance and the detectives could not think of any new questions to ask or avenues to explore.

"The funeral is the day after tomorrow. Do you think we should go or give the family their privacy?" James didn't like to intrude upon the family's time of grief, but did express a concern that something might happen between Maria and Andrew. They decided to send a plainclothes person to observe from a distance and only to interfere if a fight erupted.

Chapter 20 - One More Suspect

The following day James and Jessica went to interview the final two people. The detectives showed up on the doorstep of Norma's house located in an older neighborhood just outside of downtown. The house was beige block with lots of mature trees. The door was answered by Daniel, Andrew's brother, who was very surprised to see the detectives. James told him their purpose for being there, and the shock was very real on Daniel's face.

"I had no idea. Brenda, Mom, and I left the wedding and came home around 9:30. We did not discuss the wedding at all. Mom wanted to think about good things, like sharing time with her friend. We did discuss that Grandma seemed very out of it at the wedding. It was as if she was in a fog. Mom and I recognize when Grandma has mini strokes and we know she had one that day."

James presented the usual questions of arrival time, any special events, and Daniel's opinion of the bride and groom.

"We arrived about 30 minutes before the wedding, left about 9 p.m. There were still a lot of guests but the usual events like dancing, cutting the cake, and garter throw were over. Andrew is an asshole and made a big show of how rude he is at Mom's expense, as usual. I was glad when we could leave. Andrew didn't give seat assignments to Mom and I like he did for everyone else. I was seated in the next room, not with the family, but my table was a lot more fun. All in all, it was rejection day for his family, and we really don't care anymore. Mom spent most of the time on the dance floor with David. He's a really nice guy and they have a lot of fun together. Mom likes the exercise that goes along with dancing. David tried to teach me, but I don't have much rhythm and don't really enjoy it.

Mom changed the locks on the house the very next day. She already planned to do so because Andrew has this habit of taking whatever he wanted from the house without asking. Mom didn't trust Doreen and figured Andrew would give Doreen his key sometimes. Mom is the most loving, patient person in the world, but even I knew that Andrew had stepped over the line regarding what verbal abuse Mom could take. Instead of being depressed about it, she has been unusually happy. She feels free of the burden of trying to please him, which she knows is impossible. She knows she didn't do anything wrong, so she has peace about the situation. I know Mom would take him back if he admitted what he did was wrong and was sorry about it, but Andrew never apologizes for anything, so that won't ever happen.

I will be very blunt. I didn't like Doreen, but I didn't hate her. She was bossy and told everyone what they should do, what to wear, and what to say. I don't think she was very intelligent, and her ideas backed up my opinion. Mom and I tried to see them when other people were around so we could limit our conversations. Nothing we said or did was right, but all we wanted was to keep the peace and get along.

I hate to cut this short but I have to leave for work. Mom is riding her bike, and when you showed up, I texted for her to come home. She should be here at any time. Could I get you to wait outside?"

Chapter 21 - The Mysterious Mother

Norma was rounding the curve going to her house on her 21-speed bike when she noticed a man and woman in suits sitting in a dark sedan by the driveway. "How odd," she said to herself, "This isn't a suit neighborhood." As she pulled into the drive, the two exited the vehicle and started toward her. The yard of the ranch-style house in an older neighborhood had two large oaks creating plenty of shade. Norma had landscaped with rocks and mulch circling the two trees, small statues, a bird bath, and two benches. The area was a great place to entertain guests and where the neighbors could see her, so Norma invited them to have a seat. She didn't like the idea of strangers entering her home while she was alone.

"I'm Detective James Murphy," said the good looking, tall, slim man. He looked to be in his late

40's, but in top physical condition. Handsome would be an appropriate word, with high cheek bones, piercing blue eyes, and blond hair. "This is Detective Johnson," waving his hand toward the smaller but strong-looking, young woman. Norma guessed her to be in her mid-30's, with dark brown hair and eyes, about 5 feet 4 inches, about a size 10 but no fat, all muscle. She must spend a lot of time in the gym, Norma thought. She wasn't classically beautiful but certainly attractive enough that she would turn heads when she walked into a room of men.

Norma said hello and offered them a seat on the bench. "Isn't this a beautiful place to sit? I'm out here so much even the birds and squirrels don't run away when I come out."

"We are here about your daughter-in-law," the man said but then paused.

"Supposed daughter-in-law," Norma corrected him with a smile.

"Supposed?" he asked, realizing the conversation might take a road he didn't expect.

Norma explained, "The State of Florida says a notary or a minister authorized by a church can marry someone. In most denominations, the right to marry comes with an appointment to a church. I know a United Methodist minister can't marry someone after they retire. I was told the minister was retired from the Baptist church, and if he was an independent Baptist minister, then he didn't have the right to marry someone unless employed by the church. I don't know how the rules work for Southern Baptist or if this man was a notary. I really don't care to be honest." Norma looked startled suddenly and asked "Is my son ok? She hasn't done something to my son already, has she?"

Both detectives opened their mouths in surprise, taken back by the response. "Why would you say that?" asked Murphy.

"Because she isn't a nice person, and someday I anticipate her doing something to my son. You said you were here because of her."

Murphy bluntly said, "I'm afraid Doreen is dead. Your son hasn't told you she was in a coma at the hospital?" Again, the detective's voice showed surprise.

This questioning certainly was taking an unusual turn. The surprised look on Norma's face couldn't have been an act. She sat looking at him as if there was something else he should add. It was a couple of minutes before Norma found her voice, but there were no tears or sorrow in her eyes, only surprise. "What happened?"

James decided he had to tell the whole story for

the conversation to proceed. "On the night of the wedding, the bride drank a mixture of drugs and alcohol. She went into a coma and lasted a little over a week before she died. It was ruled an accident, but Doreen's mother is at the station every day saying her daughter wouldn't take drugs. She claims it has to be murder, so we decided we better check into it a little more thoroughly before closing the case. Do you know if Doreen ever did drugs? Why didn't your son call you to let you know?" Norma just sat silent, so James encouraged her by saying, "Your turn. We're not here to accuse anyone of murder but we would like to know what you think. I do have to tell you that you are not obligated to answer, but we would appreciate it if you would give us your opinion."

Norma had pulled out her phone and was texting. James wanted to scold her for being so rude but before he could say anything, she turned the phone off and turned back to the detectives.

Norma was an honest person, even to a fault. She had nothing to hide so she answered, "My son and I always had a difficult time communicating with each other. We see things from a different point of view. He has a tendency to think my words have hidden meaning, so when I say a sentence, he fills in what he thinks I'm really saying. I don't play games and say exactly what I think as a general rule. At the wedding, I was upset when the bride refused to have a picture taken with members of my family, like my mother and her boyfriend of forty years, who I know gave them quite a nice size check. I also thought it would be nice to take pictures with my stepmother and her boyfriend. My dad died seven years ago. About a year ago, Sandra started seeing this really nice man. The two drove all the way from Virginia to be here and she wouldn't even speak to them. My sister and her husband also traveled to be here and gave a check of a sizable amount, and Doreen was too good to have pictures with them also. My upset showed even though I tried to control it and my son, without even asking what was wrong, acted like a monster to me. We haven't spoken since I left the wedding that evening. Since he hasn't called, I assume that is the way it will stay."

Even with all this bad news, Norma still had a calm and peaceful way about her. She wasn't the type James would normally be attracted to, but he did appreciate the fact that she was not overly emotional and chose her words carefully.

Norma continued, "I really didn't know Doreen that well because she chose to keep a distance, and I respect people's decisions. We were together on holidays and special occasions at the nursing home where my mother lived, mostly having a meal. We would meet at the free concerts they have downtown on occasion, that way we were together but not. Daniel and I stood next to Andrew and Doreen, but because of the music, we didn't have to talk. Every time we were together, Doreen complained of headaches. I figured it was a manipulating lie in order to control when they would leave or to get attention. She did like to be the martyr. She would turn her head to the right and lift her chin to the air. Her hand would be on her chest placed above the breast and below the neck. She had poses, as I call them, when she would convey her emotions like a drama on a stage. She would usually say something like, 'I have such a headache but I came anyway,' or, 'I'm here when I really should be with my family,' then expected you to thank her for the sacrifice she was making. At first I did, but after a year of this act, I just ignored her like I didn't notice. When people have really bad headaches, usually there is a fog-like look in their eyes. I didn't think she really suffered from headaches because her eyes were very clear and bright, but maybe she did. I wouldn't know if she took anything for them. The only reason I don't think she did drugs is she never seemed spaced out or not paying attention to every word said. I think Doreen liked to be in control of not only herself, but everyone else around her. If you are on medication, sometimes you can't do that. The real answer is, I don't know. What did Andrew or her family say about the drugs?"

"You didn't really like her, did you?" Detective Johnson asked.

"I honestly wanted to," said Norma, "but she made it clear what my role would be in her life. Doreen felt like anyone outside of her family was an outsider. A favorite line she would say was 'Obviously, you have no clue,' which she said to me often and yet every time she said it, she was wrong. I considered that very disrespectful. I would have embraced having a daughter-in-law to spend time with, but I am perceptive and I know she didn't want me to be close. I was even willing to accept that limited role, but her actions at the wedding proved that I was to have no role. If my son hadn't been so horrible, I would have continued trying to make things work, but now I just don't care. I try not to hate anyone, but there are some people I prefer not to be around, and she was quickly becoming one of those people."

"When someone dies, people don't want to say what they really think, but only good things. They make the person out to be so perfect, which isn't always the truth. Unless you have anything to add, we thank you for being honest. Here is my card. If you think of anything that can help, please call. We may be in touch again," James said.

Norma's phone made a sound indicating a text came in. She held the phone out to James. He read where Norma had texted, 'I just found out about Doreen. Do you want me to come over? Can I do something?' The text that came from Andrew was 'No, stay away!' Murphy felt very hurt for Norma's sake. Even if he had only talked to her for a few minutes, he could find nothing negative, only a positive person. When he looked into Norma's eyes, there was sadness but her mouth was smiling and in a positive tone of voice said, "I guess we have an answer. Come back if I can be of further help." Norma turned and walked into the house.

Chapter 22 - A Second Meeting

Norma was hard at work on Friday morning when her cell phone rang. The number was not listed in her contacts but with all the calls from the nursing home and doctor offices, Norma answered even if she didn't really want to be disturbed. "This is Detective Murphy. When we talked the other day, you offered to be of further help if you could. I don't want to disturb your work day but wondered if we can meet for dinner after work."

"I go to the nursing home every night," Norma replied. "I suppose we could meet at the Good Steaks near the highway at exit 25 at around 5:15, if that's ok with you? Do you take all your suspects to dinner or am I the rare exception?" Murphy laughed and said he would be outside the restaurant when she arrived.

Norma ordered her usual soup and salad.

Murphy got a steak dinner. He began the conversation on a personal note. "I saw you riding your bike and now eating sensibly. Are you trying to lose weight?" He realized he sounded mean after the words came out, but he liked his women to be tall and skinny with bleached blonde hair. He told himself again he really was not interested in Norma, but it was just the peace that surrounded her.

Norma laughed. "I've been on a diet my whole life. Some people are just not born as skinny minis. I've been a large size since I was thirteen, and with age it is getting harder and harder to keep the weight off. I'm really doing all this working out for myself, not to impress someone else. Every year, my company does a blood workup as a part of our wellness plan, and my numbers are so bad it is scary. I don't want to end up in a hospital or nursing home, so I'm making every effort to keep fit. I work out at least three times a week, but prefer more. Mom's care takes a lot of time, so I don't have much time to spare."

Murphy knew Norma's routine of being at the nursing home daily, but didn't understand why.

Norma continued, "The nursing home does an excellent job, but you have multiple people providing care. They have never spotted when she has what I call a mini-stroke. They have new people not used to all of Mom's difficulties and I feel it is necessary to go up every night to spend time with her by playing games or writing cards. I want to make sure she is put into bed in a way that she is comfortable. Mom's health can change in a few minutes timespan, so I feel better keeping track of things to catch problems immediately. I assume we are not here to talk about my weight or Mom's care."

Murphy began his questions by opening with a statement. "Many of the things I ask may seem unimportant, but let's face facts. The crime scene was totally gone before we were called in, so all I have to work with are what people tell me. The truth is, short of a confession or an eye witness, there isn't much to go on. I don't feel most people are being honest with me, except you. I won't disclose everything that has been said to me, but will ask you in a general way to see if you can confirm or stop speculation of the things that I've been told."

He continued, "I interviewed your mother today." This got a negative look and reaction from Norma. "I don't think she understood who I was or what I was asking. Did you tell her about Doreen?"

Norma shook her head no, "I will tell her, but she is still not up to par yet. It might be stressful. Did you tell her?"

James shook his head no, "I told her I was just

visiting and heard she went to a wedding. That was enough to hear some description, but I swear she must have been at a different wedding than everyone else I interviewed. Is your mother ok mentally? Don't take that wrong, but she did seem confused and spoke with great conviction on everything she said, but her story didn't add up. She described Maria as wearing three different dresses and then leaving and returning. She said she never saw your ex-husband and his girlfriend when I know they were there. Don't take it wrong, I do like her. She reminds me of you."

Norma's eyes went wide, but James couldn't tell if she was angry or what she would say. "You really know how to make friends and impress people, don't you? First you say I'm fat and that I should diet, then you insinuate that my mother is crazy and I'm like her! Do you dislike me or do you totally lack communication skills? A must in your profession, I would think."

James cheeks flushed, "I didn't mean that. I'm so sorry. My skills do seem to disappear when I'm around you. What I meant to say is that your mom seems to look on the bright side of things, even though a lot of people in her position would be bitter or distraught. She says positive things and compliments, and says thank you to those taking care of her whenever possible. She has this aura of calm and peace that most people lack. I wasn't implying that you were crazy."

Norma decided to let him off the hook this time. "All the things you said about Mom are true. She really finds joy in everything that she can. She seldom gets upset, and I feel so helpless when she does. Mom doesn't have Alzheimer's or a disease like that. The strokes at first affected only her physical abilities like motor skills, but lately they've started to affect her mind as well. When Mom can't remember something, without realizing what she is doing, she figures out what probably happened and then believes it, even if it is nowhere near the truth. We play Mom's favorite game, Skip-Bo, almost every night. You have to play cards in stacks going from one to twelve, and she can't even do that now. She still wants to play so I play both her hand and mine."

"That would make it easy to win, wouldn't it?" James said laughing.

Norma was laughing too. "I have a strategy when I play my cards, so now I just apply that strategy to both hands. For the first time ever, she is winning. Then she calls up her friends and family to brag about how much she is beating me." Both continued to laugh, making the error of his conversation a thing of the past.

"Have you talked to the doctors? Have they

said anything about declaring her incompetent?" After the words left his mouth, James wondered if that was another mistake.

Norma didn't appear to take offense, "No," she said. "I had all the proper paperwork arranged years ago like Power of Attorney and Living Wills. I had my name on all her accounts like checking and savings. When someone is judged as incompetent, you have to get the court's permission for any action, which is time consuming, expensive, and a real hassle. I have things set up so everyone knows I make the decisions, not her, and I have the power to do so. If they try to get her to make a decision, she defers to me so having Mom declared incompetent isn't necessary and won't happen."

"Look, I hate to be rude, but I really must be going. I know you have other people's comments to discuss, so maybe we can meet another time. Do you work tomorrow? "James shook his head no. "You don't happen to like hockey, do you?"

James nodded his head yes with a grin, "Blue liner for the University of Minnesota," he said proudly.

Norma was justly impressed. "Wow, you must be good because that is a tough University to get on the team. My company has sets of season tickets to my favorite Florida hockey team due to having an office in that area. I won two tickets today at work.

I have someone to look in on Mom, thinking Daniel and I deserved the night out, but he already has plans with his girlfriend. Would you like to make a day of it and head over to the game?"

Nothing could have pleased James more, "Sure, I would love to go but let me pay for dinner. The way the traffic is, it might take an hour to get there, but it might take three, so I'll pick you up at 3:00. If we get there early, we can have dinner and if we get there late, we can have popcorn. I'm looking forward to it."

Norma walked out feeling happy and really looking forward to the game as well.

Chapter 23 - Game Day

Norma locked the door before heading to the black sedan in the driveway. She got in the car and wished James a good afternoon. He responded, but there wasn't a happy tone in his voice.

"What's wrong?" asked Norma.

"Nothing," said James, but he could tell Norma wasn't buying that. "I had a few words with Jessie, and it is a little irritating."

"Who's Jessie?" Norma persisted. "Look, if you have a girlfriend that objects, please let me know. I can get someone else to go and we can talk another time. I would hate to cause a problem."

"Jessie is my partner, Detective Jessica Johnson. She feels that I should treat you more like a suspect and that going to a game with you is unprofessional," a frowning James explained.

Norma started laughing and tried to quit, but the laughter would start all over again. "You have to admit the humor in this, the Jessie James law enforcement team."

A smirk came to James' face. "Please don't start with the jokes. We have heard them all. There is no way you will come up with something new."

"Can I at least try? I can be very witty," Norma pleaded. James just shook his head no so Norma thought it would be better to change the conversation.

"Here is the deal. You can ask me anything except during the game. Then we need to focus on having fun."

James already had his strategy worked out. He planned to talk about less personal matters in order to not ruin the day, but would wait to ask about her son until on the way home. "Let's start light. It was my understanding that Doreen's biological father showed up after being invited by Andrew. What can you tell me about that?"

"Andrew has a habit of misreading what someone else is saying. He reads more into it than what is really there. Doreen told him how upset she was at being deserted by her father. Even though she didn't remember much about him, Doreen had rules like 'Don't wear this color' or 'wear your haircut that way' because it was something she remembered her father wore or did. Andrew took this to mean she missed and longed for her dad. I didn't take it that way, but Andrew asked me to try to locate him.

Maria and Juan owned a house in town. I pulled and read their divorce from the official records and saw where they agreed to sell their house. About 6 months after the divorce, there is a deed recorded with Juan and his new wife, and Maria with her new husband, conveying the property to a third party. The document had their addresses. Juan's was an apartment, and Maria's is where she currently lives. The first name of Juan's wife was very unusual so it was easy to go to myflorida.com and look up the name in almost all the counties in Florida. I got lucky and found a match in the northeast part of the state. Then I pulled the property appraiser's information to get the mailing address. I didn't think it was a good idea, but Andrew did, and so I did what I was asked. I saw Dolly come down and order him away. I think he left."

James, maybe saying more than he should, explained, "Juan did leave and drove straight home. He stopped for gas paying by credit card. The station was about 30 miles away, and the time on the receipt proved he drove straight there from the wedding location. We interviewed the wife, who confirmed the time he arrived home, which matched the length of time to drive from the gas station to the house. Even though Maria wanted him to be a suspect, it just wasn't going to happen. Mostly, I was curious as to why he happened to be there. I'm really quite impressed with your knowledge on how to use the public records.

Next topic, the interview we had with David White, your dance partner, was interesting. He told us about his and Andrew's conversation about the job website that Doreen claimed was down. Andrew was trying to find out if you knew about it before the wedding. David said you knew and was surprised that you didn't tell Andrew. Can you give me your explanation about what happened? If you knew that Doreen had told your son a major lie, why you didn't tell your son the truth?"

It was Norma's turn to think about a story she would prefer to forget. "There is no need to tell you about the story of the system failure since you got an accurate description from David. I confirmed this fake unemployment story not just through David but from other employees I know that worked at the complex. All of them verified that the computers never went down. To tell Andrew that I thought Doreen lied would create a major riff between them and me, one that I might not be able to mend. If it was proven true, I would be at fault for destroying their relationship. My son would not blame her for lying, but me for telling him. I don't know if you spent much time interviewing Andrew, but the truth is he doesn't have true perspective of reality. I figured he would find out eventually, then I would act surprised and be the supportive mom helping him get away from her. To add to the complication of the situation, Andrew didn't tell me about Doreen not working when that happened, which was before the save-the-date announcements were sent out. Doreen sat around doing nothing but running up credit card debt for a couple months before he told me about her being unemployed. He asked me to give him $1,500.00 to pay her credit card bill because he doesn't like having debt. I said 'Not just no, but hell no!' I pointed out that she was living in his house, was driving a car he gave her, and had no need to spend money. He defended her by saying she had expenses. I taught my children to take responsibility for their actions. I am very generous with my sons if they need help, but I will not allow myself to be used and certainly didn't want to set precedence. I did give him a little cash as a gift for his birthday instead of a present, but made it clear that was a one-time thing and it would only be gifts from then on, never money."

"David told me that he never met Andrew before and seldom sees Daniel. I was wondering why when you have a relationship with David, you didn't have your sons meet him before."

James was fishing to see Norma's status more so than for the investigation. This was not missed by Norma who played along. "Where did you interview David, at his home?" James nodded yes. "Was Beth sleeping?"

James turned to look at her.

Norma continued, "Beth is David's wife. She was hurt in a car accident. She and I are good friends. She asked me to become David's dancing partner because she knows how much he loves dancing and teaching. She also knows she can trust me, where she might not be able to trust someone else. Rather than ask David to give up what he loves, she asked him to select me as his partner for the classes he teaches. I'm willing to do that because it's fun and good exercise and it solves their problems."

"Maybe," was James' only reply.

James was clearly ready to change topics, asking Norma to discuss the other family members. "Did anyone in your family feel close to Doreen? What was their opinion of Doreen and the marriage?"

Norma wanted James to talk more, hoping he would give a hint about what he learned when questioning other people. She actually preferred not to do all the talking, but felt obligated to do so since this trip was supposed to be helping with the investigation. "Mom was the only one who spent much time with Doreen. She actually felt sorry for her and would often say you can't blame Doreen for her lack-of-upbringing. She believed Doreen was basically a good person and seemed to make Andrew happy, and that's all she cared about. Mom told me one day when Andrew and Doreen were visiting that Doreen made the comment that she was afraid she would be pregnant in a few months after getting married. Mom pointed out that there were pills to help with that problem. Doreen claimed the pill didn't work for women in her family, claiming her own mother got pregnant twice while on the pills. Mom felt Doreen was laying the ground work for an excuse if she did come up expecting a child. Andrew stopped playing with his phone long enough to stare at Doreen, who quickly recovered to say it probably wouldn't happen so soon."

James made the decision to share more with Norma. "It's not common knowledge yet, but it did happen."

"What happened?" Norma's reply was very uninterested.

"Doreen was pregnant when she died. She was only a few weeks along but she was definitely with child."

The look of shock covered Norma's face. "Who knew?" she asked in a very shaky voice.

"I told Andrew, and the doctors told her mother. They were as shocked as you are. No one admits to knowing before the wedding. It really isn't a secret since we don't even know there was a murder."

Norma surmised, "That makes it even less likely that Doreen took any drugs knowingly since the baby was in her plans. I'm surprised she even drank anything with alcohol."

The news sent Norma's investigating skills into overdrive. Norma was never a professional at crime solving, but certainly had a deducting mind. "It's possible she didn't know yet herself. You have to be so many weeks along before the over-the-counter pregnancy test can work."

James was being even more logical than Norma. "Let's get back to the family members if you don't mind."

"Sandra, Daryl, Frank, and Mitch to my knowledge never had a chance to meet Doreen. I don't think they even spoke to her on the phone. My friend Brenda joined us once for a dinner we were giving for Mom on her birthday. I told Brenda that Doreen faked a headache regularly in order to have an excuse to leave, get attention, and control the gathering as much as possible. Sure enough, Doreen didn't disappoint us and began the 'poor me' show. Brenda, who is overly extraverted, decided to have some fun by asking questions seriously and with much concern. How often did Doreen get headaches? Did she think she should see a doctor? Maybe it was more than a headache since they happen so often. Maybe Doreen had a brain tumor? I kept a straight face even when Doreen turned to Andrew and said the headache was real bad now and they needed to leave. I admit the remaining guests at the dinner all joined in the laugh when the coast was clear.

My sister, Madelyn, saw Doreen about three times. She lives out of state but comes often to visit Mom. She was here when Doreen was first introduced to the family. There was a big age gap between Doreen and Andrew. When that was pointed out, she explained that they would make a good couple anyway because she was so mature for her age and Andrew was so immature. It got a laugh from everyone, which Doreen took as agreement. I took the whole conversation as a sign of disrespect, not only for my son, but to me. I expressed this to Andrew later but he blew it off as unimportant.

The next time I remember us all being together was a night after the engagement. I was taking everyone to a Christmas production of the Nutcracker. Doreen, Andrew, Daniel, Madelyn, and my friend, Sue, were in the party. I was cooking dinner before the show when Doreen came in displaying the ring. We all made the proper amount of fussing over the occasion, saying congratulations, how wonderful, when is the date? After detailing the event of the proposal and explaining how much she loved her ring, she stood there explaining what she wanted to change about the ring. She wanted this edge smoothed down and a few other suggestions for making the ring more suited for her to wear. I always felt she waited until his family was there so he would have to accept her suggestions without getting angry. The sad thing is, within a few months, Andrew went around saying I made the suggestions for the ring changes instead of Doreen. Andrew told Madelyn that I am always trashing his ideas and I'm critical of him. He was upset that I embarrassed him in front of everyone. He did show the ring to me before he gave it to her and I asked if he was sure of the size. There was so much detail in the ring; it would have been hard to alter. It was so big, it would even fit in my hands, and Doreen was petite. I didn't realize she had man fingers. Andrew was clearly annoyed with me for even asking, assuring me he made sure to have his facts right, so I quickly apologized and said how lovely it was. I was very upset that I was blamed for saying the negative things about the ring, but whenever something bad is said that Andrew docsn't like, no matter who says it to him, he will blame me. I asked Madelyn if she didn't remind him that it was Doreen saying those negative comments about the ring since she was standing right there. Maddie, being very forgetful, said she totally forgot about witnessing the event at the time and didn't remind Andrew about the truth. She said she would bring it up on the right occasion to remind Andrew who said those negative things, but it wouldn't matter. Anything bad in his life is always my fault somehow.

A few days later, Maddie saw Doreen again at the Christmas Party for the family. Nothing special happened as far as I remember. Doreen was in great spirits and enjoyed the day. She retold the engagement story and showed her ring to everyone that walked into the room. She opened her gifts and gave the normal response of 'that's nice.' I don't ever recall her saying 'thank you' since I've known her. At least it was a very good party and Mom enjoyed the family gathered around."

Norma could sense a weird change in James and had no clue why. They arrived at a beautiful restaurant on a pier extending into the Gulf of Mexico. Norma gushed over the location and elegance of the establishment. James was pleased that Norma really appreciated his choice. "I know we have an agreement to not talk about the situation at the game, but I would like to extend it to dinner if you don't mind. One last thing before we go in. Did Madelyn and Brenda already return to their homes?"

Norma confirmed that they had. James was disappointed because he preferred to talk to someone face-to-face. Norma provided the phone numbers of both women. "Madelyn is easiest to reach after 7:00 and before noon on Sundays. Brenda is available after 4:00 all evenings except Tuesday and Thursday." James was glad Norma understood that all witnesses needed to be called.

Seated on the deck overlooking the water, Norma ordered fish and chips. James went with the salmon with mixed vegetables. The breeze was warm and they were still eating at the time to watch the sunset. "If we aren't talking about the case, it would be difficult to talk about me. Why don't we talk about you?" Finally, a chance to learn something about James, Norma thought to herself.

"Not my favorite topic," said James with a nervous look.

"To play for the University of Minnesota, you had to be really good. Did you ever play pro?"

"One season in the minors, I was only good

enough for the third line. I didn't care for life on the road at that time. There were more important things in my life so I gave it up. So many thugs play in the minors, taking out their frustrations of not having the skills for the big time on the players trying to work their way up. I didn't mind the pranks on the rookies, but I did get tired of getting bruised and bloody all the time. If I had the skills, I would have kept at it but knowing my limitations, I knew I didn't want to end up in the minors my entire career. I had just gotten married, and my wife was expecting, so I hung up my skates and became a small town deputy. I played on the police league until I was about 40, but decided it was better for the young guys to have their time."

"I presume you are not still married, or you wouldn't be here with me, is that right?" Norma watched his face closely to see any reaction.

James paused before replying, "I am divorced and enjoy being a bachelor."

"Do you have any children?" Norma preferred not to pry into something as personal as the divorce.

"I have four, three boys and one girl from the first marriage. The second marriage, when I was older, was just a short term situation and neither of us wanted children."

"Tell me about the children," encouraged

Norma.

"James is 29, his degree is in political science, married for five years and expecting his first child. John is 27. He went the skilled labor route because he loves working with his hands. He is a cabinet maker with long hair and a beard. He likes to joke that he is trying to follow Jesus. Sarah is 25. She married about four years ago and has a 1 year old and a 3 year old. Both are girls. She works at a book store a few nights and one day on the weekend to help with the bills and to get out of the house. She and her husband both feel it is better for one of them to be with the children instead of the expense of daycare. Timothy is the youngest. He is 20 and has Down's Syndrome. He lives with my ex-wife and her husband out in the country in northern Minnesota. His case is mild. One of the neighbors has a farm, and Tim loves working there with the animals. He is very strong and can handle most jobs on the farm, but he does have to be watched. Bob, the farmer, is great with teaching Tim and appreciates the company Tim provides. I talk to my kids every week and sometimes more, so I would say we are pretty close. They understood my need to move and even encouraged me. I left the small town for Minneapolis, worked my way up to detective. I could retire after twenty years there, so I left there knowing I would have a retirement for my old age and moved here. There is a twenty year retirement program here also, so I plan to work until I have two retirement incomes."

James enjoyed talking about his children and was very proud of them. Norma was glad not to have to carry the conversation, just listened, with the occasional question or positive comment. The dinner concluded at just the right time to leave for the game. Norma said, "I take it you are going to be cheering for the out-of-town team tonight."

James answered by his grin.

Norma continued, "That's ok, I have a policy of cheering on the home team at any arena, but tonight I'm with you for my own reasons. I just don't like offending the locals."

James was reassuring when he said "I'm not very expressive at a game. I just like seeing a good game."

Chapter 24 - The Game Is On

As James pulled into the parking garage by the arena, Norma reached into the cloth bag she brought with her and pulled out a jersey from the minor league hockey team whose games they both attended for years unknown to each other. James was a little embarrassed at Norma's choice of attire until she had it on and turned around. The back had the name of Minnesota's star player, but instead of the last name, it read "Slamming Swede," the nickname of James's favorite player. The autograph signature on the back covered half the jersey. James could not help but laugh out loud. Swede played for the Bears for a half season as he got acclimated to the U.S. and the new system of playing hockey. A star in his own country, he soon became a star in his new country.

Both felt the air of excitement as they walked

to their seats on the visitor side, lower bowl near the curve. They were early and the teams were just coming out for their pre-game warm-up. Swede looked up and saw the Bears jersey and waved with a big smile. Norma waved back. The rest of the team was waving at Norma also, with a shocked James looking on. A few minutes later, an usher approached and asked Norma if she could accompany him. They walked to the ice and the door to the ice opened a crack. Swede skated by and whispered something through the crack. Norma smiled, tilted her head forward, and Swede kissed the top of her head and skated quickly back to finish warm-ups. Norma returned to her seat and sat down. For once in his life James was speechless.

Norma turned to James, "I know it's been a long day already, but Swede and the rest of the team are spending the night at the hotel directly across the street and wondered if we could join them for a drink after the game."

James was so excited that he almost kissed Norma on the top of her head too. "Sure, I'm off tomorrow, so no problem." James wondered if he managed to look composed in spite of wanting to jump and shout a big yes. James would have loved an explanation of how Norma knew the Slammer, but one was not forthcoming.

The game commenced with the intensity of a

play-off game. Hard hits and total focus were used to send a message that since the teams only met a couple of times a year, that should they meet in the playoffs, they would be tough competition. It was late in the season and every point mattered to their placement in the playoff spot in their division. It was ten minutes into the first period when Swede got the first point for his team. The nickname "Slamming" came from the extremely strong slap shot that would rocket off Swede's stick with no telling signs that it would be coming to the goalie.

The game continued through the rest of the first period with all defense. James expressed the appreciation for a more defensive game, with the old saying that defense is what wins games. The hard hits of strong defense did make tempers flare, causing the first fight five minutes into the second period.

Norma didn't react to the fight, offering her opinion that she liked Olympic and college hockey because of the no-fighting rules. She did understand that boys will be boys, and when you get 12 men with sticks on the ice, a fight is going to be inevitable.

James was recalling a few tough fights he had been in and was grateful that getting hit was mostly in his past. Being a detective was not like on television, where you had to fight your way through every case. James could hold his own in a fight, but the strength of the men on the ice probably made them feel like they got hit by a truck the next day. The fight spurred on the hometown team, who managed to score two goals before the end of the period.

The third period continued the defense-only style of play, but with five minutes left in the third, the Minnesota team finally found the back of the net, managing to tie the game. If the first part of the game seemed hard hitting, it was only a warm up for the last five minutes. Both teams needed the points to hold position in their division. It was down to the final second and it appeared there would be overtime when Swede picked the pocket of the right winger of the Tampa team. The breakaway was a success with the shot so quick and hard that the goal didn't stand a chance.

James and Norma tried to applaud their team with a quiet respect for the disappointed fans walking with their heads down towards the exit. Norma removed the jersey, carried it folded as they exited to the hotel, knowing that it would be a long wait for the team while they showered and listened to the coach talk about the game.

A Break from the Story

"BOOOOOOOOOOOOOO!" was the chorus of the ladies listening to the story.

Belinda led the attack, "Really? No one in the world could ever tell a story of murder, mental intrigue, and possible romance then bring hockey into the story. I know it is your favorite sport but how could they have ended up at a hockey game?"

"Free tickets?" responded Jean.

"Then it is real! How else could there be free tickets?" Priscilla surmised.

Jean just grinned, "That or the author just has good taste in sports. I really don't understand your opposition to me enjoying such a fast paced and exciting game."

Eve corrected the group, "Who cares? Let's just get to the romance. If I were going to write a book, it would definitely be a love story. Nothing makes joy come to someone's heart like a romantic interlude."

Jean made an ugly face, "Speak for yourself. I would rather have a good hockey game instead of an exchange of bodily fluids."

Josephine returned a look of disgust to her sister, "Jean, you always could kill the joy of a couple being together. It's hard to believe you are dating someone. I hope he is more romantic than you are."

Jean wanted to change the subject quickly, "Let's get back to the story. I'll make sure the ending is not only happy, but one of blossoming new love just for you. No more booing or I won't finish and you will never know if justice was delivered."

Chapter 25 - Meeting the Team

Seated at a table in the bar of the hotel that gave a view of the door, Norma still didn't offer an explanation of how she knew Swede, but talked about the game in depth. The 1980 Olympic game being one of the most exciting games in history is what turned Norma into a dedicated fan of hockey. Norma admitted she didn't always cheer for Minnesota but picked the teams by the players on it, which is more of a woman's style. Norma felt men picked their team and stayed dedicated to it no matter who was on the team.

The victorious team came through the door of the hotel with plenty of smiles. Swede, a very good looking man in his late 20's, 6 feet 3 inches tall and weighed about 225 pounds, walked to the table while Norma stood up to receive her hug. James was introduced and handshakes were exchanged.

The conversation started immediately about Swede's wife and three children. It was obviously more personal than just normal inquires. Everything from school to the children's out of school activities were discussed. James just sat more as an observer since he didn't have anything to contribute to the conversation. Finally, an explanation was given that Norma was the godmother to the children and had contact with the family every week, if not more often.

Four of the other players were sitting at another table near the bar but they all came by to greet Norma. Swede was drinking milk and while Norma had one glass of wine, she also drank about two glasses of water. James was nursing his beer since he had to drive home. Norma excused herself and headed to the ladie's room. Norma was no more than a step away from the table when Swede began his line of questioning.

"So how do you know Norma? Have you been seeing Norma long? Is this a serious relationship?"

James felt he was being interrogated and said he had an opportunity to meet Norma through his work.

"What kind of work do you do?" Norma was heading back into the room but was called over for conversation with the other players.

James decided that Swede might have some insight about the players in the mystery, so James decided to be forthright about the relationship. "Norma's son Andrew was married a few weeks ago, and his wife became comatose that night and died a week later." The look on Swede's face was pure shock. Norma hadn't told him about the death of her daughter-in-law. "I'm a detective and trying to check into the death to see if it was accidental or intentional. I take it you didn't know anything about it. Were you invited to the wedding?"

Swede said, "No, I'm not close to Andrew. I'm very close to Norma and Daniel. When you said intentionally, are you saying someone murdered the girl? Are you saying you suspect Norma or her sons?"

James knew he had to tread lightly because Swede couldn't hide his anger. The hockey star was usually a mild mannered person off the ice, but it was clear that anything done or said against Norma would cause his temper to flair. "I'm not sure it was murder, but Doreen's mother is accusing everyone on Andrew's side of the family of wrongdoing. However, there is no evidence that it was anything but an accident. I had to interview Norma and actually, I liked her. She has a calm manner and seems happy and content even through adversity. She is the only one that I feel answers my questions honestly. Do you know Andrew?"

Swede asked a question that didn't seem unusual to James but would to anyone else. "Did you ever play hockey?" The nod yes confirmed it was true. "What's said in the locker room stays in the locker room. Same thing goes about family. I have nothing to say because I don't know if I can trust you. I don't like it that Norma is even with you."

James was trying to use logic, "Andrew became very ugly to his mother during the reception. I was trying to get more insight into their relationship and Andrew's attitude. Do you think Andrew could harm anyone?" James sensed that Swede didn't care for Andrew, but he still didn't say anything.

One of the players shouted across the room, "Why don't you two join us in the back room at the pool table. I think Norma should allow me a chance to redeem myself after our last meeting."

Swede shouted back, "I'll be there in a minute. Why don't you start, and I'll play the winner."

Swede, wanting to know more about Andrew's attack on Norma, decided to share information with James. "When I first came to this country with my wife and 9-month old son, I played for the Bears. At a question and answer session with the fans, Norma and Daniel were present. My wife wasn't feeling very good and Norma went over to talk to her. The only problem was my wife didn't speak English. I went over, and Norma expressed concern because she knew the team was about to go on the road for two weeks. My family was living in a monthly hotel, and there were such a concern over disturbing the other guests if the baby cried in the night. There were times when people in the other rooms were a little loud and woke the baby. I didn't like leaving them, but what else could I do? Norma invited my wife and son to use a spare bedroom in her home until my return. I politely declined because I didn't know her or what kind of person she was. She gave me her phone number and said if my wife had any problem while I was gone, to call her. I did give the number to my wife and repeated Norma's words. A couple of nights later, there were some very bad men staying in the next room. They kept knocking on the door and wanting my wife to come party with them. She called Norma but the language problem made it so they couldn't understand each other. Norma got a friend of hers named Garrett to call my wife back because he could speak our language. He told my wife to stay inside the room with the doors locked and they would be there soon. Daniel, Garrett, and Norma came over, helped my wife pack up and took her to Norma's home. Garrett gave my wife his phone number and said to call if she needed someone to translate. Norma had my wife call to tell me where she was and that she was ok. The next morning when my wife woke up, Norma had a translation machine that you type in the words of your language and it converted to another language as specified. By the time I returned, my wife was learning English and Daniel was learning Swedish, but Norma was still using the machine. My son loved Norma and would reach for her if she walked by. I knew my family was in safe hands. We moved in for the remainder of the season and have been close ever since. Norma would visit us a couple of the times during the season to help out when I traveled, especially when the other children were born. My mother died when I was in my teens and Norma became like a grandmother to my children."

James persisted, "What about Andrew? Was he around?"

Swede didn't like talking about someone behind their back but was concerned for Norma. "No, Andrew was at college at the time. I came home one day and found him yelling at Norma in the driveway. I understand he came home unexpectedly for the weekend and Norma never told him about us living in what used to be his room. He didn't like someone else using his things. Norma didn't get mad or upset, but said firmly that it was her house and she would permit whomever she wanted to stay there. Andrew could move his things out and she would go buy new stuff for us to use. Andrew got quiet when I walked up, and I told him that I would move out that day. Norma wouldn't permit it. Andrew wasn't brave enough to yell at his mother in front of me. He knew who I was and guessed it would be cool to be friends with a hockey player. He started backing down right away, saying he didn't mean I needed to move, but that his mother disrespected him by not asking his permission to let someone else use his room. It looked to me that he was disrespecting Norma speaking to her that way. He stayed the night and slept in Norma's room while she slept on the couch. Later on when I hit the big time, Andrew tried to act like my friend. I only saw him at holiday meals, and he would always want to talk about hockey. He would say bad things about various players. I wouldn't comment but just looked at him. He would say things like 'You agree with me, don't you?' I finally made it clear that hockey players keep their opinions to themselves about other players, and I would never agree or share my comments with him. He was offended but backed down again, saying he was just trying to be friendly. He used curse words at the table, and if his mother or grandmother asked him not to, he would yell at them. When I told him not to cuss in front of my children, he backed down and agreed. Andrew is a bully and likes to hurt people with words, but I don't think he would physically hurt anyone. He picks on people that he can tower over or scream louder than they do, but he's all mouth. There are times he is nice to Norma but she stays on guard because he changes moods very quickly. He gets mad when he feels that people don't show him respect, but he doesn't understand what respect is. You don't respect someone for what they accomplish or the material possessions they own. My dad was a blue collar worker all his life, but he loved his family. He was always there for us with kind words and support. I respect my father. You have to give respect to others to receive respect. Now that I shared my knowledge of the family with you, I want to know what is happening to Norma."

James told the story as he heard it not just from David, but everyone at the wedding, of how Andrew started yelling at this mother for no reason and saying she had to obey him and do everything he wanted or she would never know her grandchildren. James also disclosed that Andrew refused to see or speak to his mother but didn't specify why.

Swede just smiled and said "Norma has her grandchildren, and they love and respect her. She doesn't need someone who will teach their kids to be rude to her, or to be around someone yelling at her. So tell me honestly, do you suspect Norma or Andrew of doing this terrible thing?"

James responded, "I don't know about Andrew, but never Norma."

Swede ended the conversation with, "Norma has solved many mysteries before. You might be surprised at how helpful she could be if you trusted her with details of the case."

Norma and the teammates returned wanting to know why Swede and James had not joined them. Swede just said, "I need to question him to see if I approve of you being with him."

The coach came into to the bar and ordered his team to their rooms. James and Norma headed for the long drive home.

Chapter 26 - The True Relationship

Norma apologized as they got in the car, "I guess I should have told Swede about what happened, but I just didn't want to worry him. He really cares about me."

James would have preferred to end the night with nice conversation, but he was here to investigate so he decided to put the happy feelings aside and asked pertinent questions. "Swede doesn't seem to like Andrew, but he doesn't believe Andrew would kill someone. Swede knows how to read a person which is why he is such a great hockey player, besides his powerful slap shot. I have to ask you about your son and also try to understand why he dislikes you so much."

Norma was hurt with that statement, but she didn't shy away from the truth. "I agree with Swede. Andrew is a bully but he would never hurt someone physically. Even with the discovery that his wife was a liar, he married her anyways but knowing him, he would have held a grudge about that lie. It would have been brought up regularly during disagreements but he wouldn't kill over it. You said that he didn't know about Doreen being pregnant, and if anything, even though he didn't want children yet, he would have been even more protective because he would have instantly loved and protected the child. While my son likes to control everyone, and he likes to put others down to make himself feel superior, he is not a killer.

As far as his dislike of me, he was brought up being taught that I was a liar and a horrible person by his father. I thought that never saying anything bad about his father and being the best mom I could be would be enough to show him what his father taught him wasn't true, but it didn't happen that way. I was the one who raised him, taught him right from wrong, and was by his side not only for the fun things like scouts and little league games, but there to help him when things went wrong. His father would never bail him out of financial difficulty. His father dropped him from health care coverage, even though it was no additional expense, just because he wanted to be cruel. The supposed wonderful father knew I would add Andrew to my coverage at a huge expense as long as I could because I gave up everything for my children, including time and money."

Norma wanted to end there but could tell James wouldn't let it go, so she chose to continue. "Children are born with their own personalities, but that can be molded and shaped especially in the first two years of their lives. Andrew was born controlling and selfish. I even wrote in his baby book at about six months that he was happy as long as he got his own way. For his first two years, I lived with his father. I was cursed at daily with four letter words and told the only reason he was with me was because of Andrew. I would cover Andrew's ears and try to be soothing to hide the negativity, but there was still a huge impression that his mother could be yelled at for no reason. If I visited my family, the insults would be even worse because I was told on my honeymoon that I was never to have contact with my family again. He tried to make it so I didn't even get a house key, but that didn't work out. Any murder or rape story would be read aloud and I was told if I left the house, the same thing would happen to me. I finally realized that living in poverty and alone was the only hope to raise Andrew in a loving home. During the divorce, the court required counseling by a therapist who taught us how to parent for the best interest of the child.

As I said, Andrew has a way of looking on the

negative and my ex would ask questions like 'How are you and your mother getting along? How are things at your house, son?' After Andrew would complain, his father would say, 'That's the way your mother is, or your mother should consider you first.'

We had a good life until I made the decision to have another child. I never wanted to get married again but did want another child. I told Andrew that this baby could be his best friend in the world, but he was so jealous that he would kick Daniel or be mean to him whenever he could.

At the age of 15, Andrew was so horrible to live with, and for every problem in his life, he blamed it on the fact that he was raised without his father. I supported the idea for him to go live with his dad. I offered to pay the travel to his father's home and give the same child support I received. He called his dad saying he wanted to live with him and told him about my offer. I was handed the phone and was asked if I was going to make Andrew a ward of the court if he didn't take him. I said no and his dad said, 'I won't let my son go into the system, but if you aren't kicking him out, I don't want him here. I am a much desired man with many girlfriends and can't have him cramping my style. You wanted him, so you got him.' I told him to tell Andrew that and he said he would tell Andrew what he wanted, but it would do no good for me to tell Andrew what he said because he taught his son that I was a liar and he would deny that he was refusing to take him. After that, when I handed the phone back to Andrew, I could hear a few comments on my end. After he hung up, I asked Andrew when he was going to leave. Andrew told me his father said I needed him and he needed to stay and be a man for me. I reminded Andrew that he heard me say it was alright to go and if he didn't, it was not my fault. Andrew shouted, 'Yes, it is!' as he stomped off.

Things got worse when Andrew turned 18 and child support was no longer due. His dad made promises to Andrew only to not fulfill them. He wrote letters to Andrew in which the first page talked about what a good father he was. The second page was what he wanted Andrew to do. Andrew was a good son if he followed the instructions and a bad son if he didn't. Then there were two pages of what a horrible person I was. Andrew's girlfriend at the time would cry when she read them. She made copies of the letters and gave them to me. I showed them to Detective Sims, and he said that if my ex came near me, I could get a restraining order because the man was crazy.

After Andrew moved out of the house, we could get along during family occasions like birthdays and holidays, but you never knew when he would exhibit extreme mood swings. Mom and Daniel can verify that for you. We all questioned if he might have bipolar disorder. Every time Andrew got a girlfriend who he thought he would marry, he would start screaming at me, telling me how much he hated me and that once he married, I would never see him again. This actually happened a few times, so I wasn't surprised that it happened again, but I was surprised that it was so public and that he ruined his own wedding."

James really felt sorry for Norma. She spoke with a very unemotional tone, but he was sure she was hurt. He had asked Andrew about his mother and saw for himself the rage and hate contained in the man. James had also discussed the relationship with a couple of others that knew both of them and everyone said the same thing, that Norma was a good mom and Andrew was just filled with hate for her.

James tried to think of something to say to help soothe Norma's hurt feelings, "You really seem to be a happy and calm person in spite of all that you have been through."

"I try to live by the 'Serenity Prayer,'" said Norma. "I depend on the strength that God provides to help me through the hard times and what I must tolerate. I always try to look for the joy on all occasions. I'm very strong in my faith and know

God loves me and wants me to be happy. I turn Andrew over to God in my prayers every night, but unless Andrew apologizes, admits his wrong treatment of me and assures me that it won't happen again, I plan to just back off and let God be his guide. I believe being happy and enjoying life is a choice that we can make daily. Sure, there are always bad things that happen, but if you look on the positive side and count your blessings, things will work out ok. I truly have total peace with the situation because I did everything I could the best I could, so I have no regrets."

About this time, the hockey fans arrived at Norma's house. Norma's exit was a bit of a surprise because she ended with, "Swede also told you I have solved mysteries in the past, and it's true, murders in fact. I look at the truth not as an optimist or a pessimist, but just the facts. I believe Doreen was murdered, and I believe you are looking at the wrong family to find the guilty party."

Chapter 27 - The Story of James

The late hour of their return was the reason James waited until 11:00 to call Norma the next day. "Hi, you sure left me with a surprise ending last night. What are your plans for today?" was his opening line.

Norma had mixed feelings, being glad to talk to James yet thinking to herself that she didn't have time for a man in her life. Norma replied, "Sunday's routine is to work out at the gym, then go to the nursing home and bring dinner for Mom."

James had no intentions of going away easily, "May I buy dinner and go with you to see your mom?" Norma finally consented but with a warning that she would signal if she thought the conversation would upset her mother, and he had agreed to change the subject if indicated.

The patio area in the back of the nursing home

was very pleasant with a gazebo covering the table and chairs, surrounded by a garden with lovely flowers as nature's bouquet. The meal was tacos, which was Betty's request. Betty, who seemed to be of good mind and spirits, was leading the conversation with questions about James, his family and history. Norma said, "I told you all about my marriage last night. It's your turn now."

James was reluctant but relented, telling his story to Betty about his hometown, family, hockey career, college and marriage life, along with the details of all his children.

Norma asked the question he didn't want to answer, "Why did you get divorced?"

James appreciated that Norma had been straightforward last night and decided to trust her with the rest of his story. "Basically, it was no one's fault about the divorce. I didn't want to have so many children because we couldn't afford them. When Tim was born, I had no choice but to work extra hours to cover medical bills and tests. Tim required one of us to be with him all the time. My wife didn't work so I took on extra hours, usually working sixteen hours a day. It might be security at an event, night watchman, or just additional shifts. I was exhausted most of the time with only a quick meal and a few hours to sleep at home. My best friend since grade school, Josh, and his wife, Amy, were a great support. Josh took my place with the kids little league games and scouts. They didn't have any children and truly enjoyed interacting with mine. All was going well until Amy got cancer. It really wasn't that long from the discovery until she died. It was my wife's opinion that she should be a support to Josh during this difficult time."

Norma was nodding her head like she already knew where this was headed. "In the end, they fell in love with each other. Since Josh was already acting like the father of the house, the kids not only accepted it but welcomed the idea of him becoming their dad. Josh received a lot of insurance money so he was now well off. When they approached me about the divorce, an offer was made where I didn't have to pay child support. I could go back to working a normal schedule and have more time with the kids to build a relationship with them. I talked to the children and it was clear that this was what they wanted too. We got divorced, and on the outward appearance it looked like the perfect friendship with me and the newlyweds. Inside, I was devastated to lose my family and be the outsider in this new life. I took the offer of no child support and instead set up college funds for all of them. Tim wouldn't be going to college but I gave equally to his account so there would be money to help him in whatever way was needed."

Norma looked up with realization on her face, "That's why you got so upset when you found out that David was married yet dancing with me. Did you automatically assume I would do something with David like what happened to you?"

James flushed and fumbled for the right thing to say, "Norma, you can see the similarity between the two. I didn't automatically think you would cheat with David, but considering my past, you can see why the situation made me a little edgy." Norma decided to let it go. After all, there wasn't anything between her and James.

Betty changed the conversation to stories of her home town and family, which James and Norma appreciated hearing. James really enjoyed the evening. He waited outside while Norma went in and helped the staff prepare her mother for bed. When Betty was comfortable and prepared to watch a little television before going to sleep, James and Norma left.

In the car, James flipped on an oldies station and listened to the Moody Blues singing 'Tuesday Afternoon.' "I love that CD," said Norma. "This is horrible to say but I think 'Nights in White Satin' is the sexiest song ever recorded. I always wanted to make love to that song but it never happened and never will."

"Why not?" asked James.

"I gave up sex twenty years ago." Norma stated.

"Why? How could you do that?" asked James in an astonished tone of voice.

"I taught bible school and one of the students said she couldn't wait to get married, even if she got divorced so she could have sex. She said her parents told her that was the way it worked. I told her I didn't think so, but I limited what I said because I didn't want to discredit her parents. It made me take a look at myself, even though after the divorce my dating activities were very limited and I never brought a man home to meet my sons. I knew I wanted a closer relationship with God, so I had to practice what I preached, so I just quit dating. My sons wanted a dog. I used to have the most perfect dog in the world and couldn't face losing another one. I told my sons that we should pray about it, 'God, if you want us to have a dog, leave the perfect one on our doorstep.' My sons got mad and said that wasn't fair. Two weeks later, the perfect dog was on the doorstep when we got home. The kids jumped from the car saying there is the dog we prayed for. That dog was a part of our life for the next fourteen years. I told God if he wanted me to be with someone in my life that he would have to put the perfect man on my doorstep, and it never happened." James thought that was a little weird to give up relationships but admired Norma's dedication to her faith.

It was a good time to change the conversation, so James brought the subject back to the ending sentence of last night, "Do you think someone in Doreen's family killed her? If so, why? Are you holding out any information?"

Norma gave a chuckle. "I've always been very observant all my life. I'm not the type to watch crime shows on TV but the kind that reads Nero Wolfe stories by Rex Stout or Agatha Christie books like Miss Marple. I watch people, observing not only what they say but their actions as well. Doreen's family will tell you how close they are and how much they love each other, but the truth is Maria pitted the girls against each other so they had to fight for attention and approval. I was around Maria three times, the dinner, the shower, and the wedding, but I noticed no one ever spoke to Maria except when needed, and even then it was not in friendly conversation. No one in my family had a reason to kill Doreen. I wanted to like her. We had some things in common such as our taste in movies and music. My hope at the time was for her to overcome her negative mindset so we could work on building a friendship. I stayed away in order to give both of them space. I went along with their every request. If she had lived and had my son not been such a jerk, I would have gone over more and treated them with kindness.

Andrew wouldn't have killed her because he wanted to be married and planned to change her way of thinking to fit his own.

Doreen was after Andrew for his money and didn't realize he spent every dime he earned. She was so intent to separate him from the people at the family table, all of whom actually had a great deal of money. The irony was Andrew would have inherited money from four of the people that couldn't be photographed. But after Doreen and Andrew's actions at the wedding, all four people altered their wills so Daniel will inherit everything and Andrew will receive nothing."

James pushed on, "Do you have any idea who did it?"

Norma was very serious when she said, "You have me doing all the talking. I have to learn what they have said and the exact cause of death to determine if I know who did it. I have had many experiences with crime in the past but not on your level. I have been the one to have a few observations, but without more facts, I can't put it all together."

They were at the house and James said, "Can I come in and discuss more of what you saw? I know you are sick of talking about this, but I am being pushed to rule whether it was accidental or a homicide. If it's the latter, I need to produce a murderer. The boss is pushing that by Friday of next week to either solve the case or put it in the dead case file. I should get the test results back the Monday of next week as to the exact cause of death. The other interviews are confidential but in all honesty, none have resulted with any important facts and some were outright lies. Most people won't to speak ill of the dead."

It was late and with work the next day, Norma put him off by saying she would be glad for him to join her after work for dinner and the nursing home if he could get away.

Norma got out and headed to the door when impulsively James jumped from the car and walked her to the door. "I really enjoyed the past couple of days," he said with sincerity. "I just want to remind you of one thing. I was sitting on your doorstep when you came home." He opened the door, gave her a hug and walked to the car with a spring in his step.

Norma just stared, feeling not only confused but with a sense of discomfort. Her life was nice and smooth. Boringly content was her description for it. She didn't know if she would ever trust a man again or even if she wanted to.

Chapter 28 - The Story Continues

Norma and James went to dinner after work with plans to go see Betty. After ordering, Norma asked a surprising question. "You seemed very honest last night about your wife and children, but what about Lisa?"

James was surprised for only a minute, knowing that Norma knew how to use the public records. "I take it you looked me up online and found out the name of my second wife. I married a second time after moving south. It's nice you care so much to make the effort."

Norma started to protest, but she had walked into that one, so she had no choice but to put up with the grin he was wearing.

"Lisa was a singer at a country bar. A lot of policemen stopped there after work. It was sexual chemistry and not much else. Hell, I don't even like country music. It was a quick romance from bed to marriage only to wake up to find we had nothing in common. Her goal was to be a star and hit the big time, and my goal was just to get by one day at a time. She was offered a recording contract that required a move to Nashville. She checked it out and decided to make the move. She told me that she thought it would be easier to live life on the road as a single person, and she didn't think a long distance marriage would work. She didn't even ask if I would consider a move to Nashville. I wouldn't have gone anyways and agreed a divorce would be the best thing. It was less than a year of marriage, no kids, and no shared assets, so we walked to the courthouse and did a short-form divorce with no attorney. It was actually a relief because I didn't care. She was a nice person. I'm not saying anything bad about her, but she didn't want to meet my kids. She didn't even have contact with her own family. I have to say that family and good values mean a lot to me, and she didn't understand that. Does that satisfy your curiosity?"

Norma just smiled and nodded yes.

"I want to ask you questions about the case. Would it be better to speak here than at the nursing home?" Norma nodded yes, but with no smile this time. "Tell me about your interaction with Doreen and her family."

Norma had various places to begin but assumed that the first time they met was as good as any. "Doreen came for dinner. I had friends and family visiting. She seemed ok, but after dinner she started talking about how mature she was and how immature Andrew was, so that covered the gap in their ages. I saw that as an attack on my son. I agree that he is immature, but if you have to tell someone how mature you are, chances are you aren't mature at all. It was close to Christmas, and I got her a lovely gift of jewelry only because I didn't know her well enough for anything else. A string of pearls are usually a hit, but she just tossed them aside saying that's nice. She found fault with each gift she unwrapped. For example, Daniel got Doreen some candy and she responded that she didn't like that brand. No matter what she received, she had a negative comment. She acted like she was so much better than everyone else and never said thank you, not even once.

Daniel took an instant dislike to her because she was always telling him what he should wear, how he should do his hair, and what he should do for a social life. The comments were not welcomed at all, and all he could say was that he would rather be single all of his life than marry someone like her.

Mom thought she was nice enough, but Mom always looked for the good side in people. If rude manners showed, she would just say that Doreen couldn't help the way she was raised. We saw them only on holidays, birthdays, or the occasional downtown concert series. Usually Doreen pretended to have a headache so she could dictate when they would leave. I really didn't care because she acted nice enough and it wasn't like I wanted to interfere with their life, so I was nice and let it go.

After the engagement, I was told to stay out of the plans. They bluntly said that they didn't want my input. I would have helped financially, but with being omitted on the decisions of how the money would be spent, I just said to tell me when and where to be, and made no offers. I know my son always wanted a wedding at the beach, which is probably why he dressed like he was going on an inexpensive boat. Doreen didn't care what he looked like because she wanted all eyes on her. I know her parents paid a little, but my son paid for most of the wedding. He spent thousands on the wedding and the ring while still owing me money. I didn't need the money, but the point was they didn't make good choices. They spent money like they had it, so I would never loan them money again. I can't say anything special stood out before the wedding plans other than the negative attitude and the constant need for approval.

She lived for free with Andrew and bragged if

she did the dishes or cooked one meal. If you didn't rave about what a great job she did or 'ooh and aah,' she would repeat the story until you made noises of approval. Then in the fall, I heard the story about Doreen not working all summer. I know David told you that story about being fired from her job. I checked it out and can tell you it was a lie and that she just chose not to work. At this time, I wanted nothing to do with her and prayed Andrew would see the truth before getting into this marriage. I interviewed four male co-workers and three of them suggested to not say anything because if Andrew told Doreen I said things against her, and they married anyways, there would be no way to have a good relationship with her. One friend said to tell the truth. I wish I would have listened to him now."

James stated, "I understand the difficulty with Doreen, but unless she did an accidental overdose, I need to hear about her family and friends."

"Friends?" Norma shook her head no. "Every now and then, she mentioned a friend or two but said that they didn't need outside friends, that family was all you needed in life. After the engagement was announced, Andrew called saying Maria wanted the parents to meet and suggested dinner for the next night. I arranged for someone to be with Mom and went to Andrew's house. Instead of dinner where we could have a nice quiet visit, we left for a restaurant / nightclub complex that Doreen and Dolly worked at to meet up with Doreen's parents. We entered only to hear Maria complaining to the kids because they didn't make reservations. They assumed the place would be available, but the whole dining room had been reserved. They talked for 15 minutes and no one spoke to me or introduced me. I started to say hello first, but I wasn't the one that called the meeting. Besides, I was curious as to how long it would take before proper manners came into play. It was Andrew that finally did the introductions after the decision was made to eat in the lounge.

Maria and Doreen took the inside seats of the booth, the men on each side with me sitting in the aisle in a chair that was not the right height for the table. I made some effort to talk with the others, but what I asked or stated was either ignored, or the ladies would try to top my story by saying something like, 'That's nothing, you should hear about what happened to me.' It was like the two women had the discussion for the evening all planned, and they executed their agenda.

At first, I talked to Maria's husband until I saw him jerk, most likely because he was kicked under the table. We talked sports and cars, not anything of importance. Andrew and I talked a little, but no one joined our conversation. At the time of ordering, the waitress was told by Doreen's stepfather that he was paying only for him and his wife. He told her he didn't know how the rest of us wanted to divide our checks. I volunteered to pay for the three of us. I know they don't have much money, but it was another case of bad manners. They could have at least paid for their own daughter.

When the check arrived, Maria walked out to the reception stand and presented it to Dolly, telling her to go ask her boss to waive the charge. The beaten Dolly went into the office and asked if there was anything he could do. She came back with the bill lowered by 40%, which was the employee discount. Maria loudly shouted that it wasn't good enough and ordered her to go back in to talk to the boss again. Dolly pretended to go around the corner into the office again, but instead when out of sight of her mother, got out her purse and went to pay the bill. Andrew, Doreen, and I came out and while Dolly took care of the bill, Andrew talked to a friend of his also working in the desk area named Doug. It appeared Andrew and Doreen were introduced at a party at Doug's house.

It was an expensive and horrible evening. It would have been nicer to cook something at Andrew's and have a nice quiet conversation. I felt no need to return the offer for dinner since I paid for my own meal and could tell that I didn't like their company. As far as I was concerned, having no more contact before the wedding would have suited me just fine."

James and Norma arrived at the nursing home, dropping all conversation of murder for a fun game of Skip-Bo and hearing the events of the afternoon. It appeared the Hooter Girls were there in the afternoon for entertainment for the men in residence, and Betty and her friend decided to crash the party, having as much fun with the young ladies as the men. Watching Jeopardy and Wheel of Fortune as they played cards showed James that not only could Norma multi-task, but did so with a competitive spirit.

Chapter 29 - A Long Day of Scheduled Interviews

James told Jessie about the past three days. They were working on other cases, so there was little need to discuss the Doreen case. James avoided confessing about the amount of time he was spending with Norma, as he knew Jessie didn't approve. After presenting all the facts minus the emotional feelings, Jessie and James decided to take a closer look at Doreen's family.

The first stop was at the restaurant where they lucked out to find Doug on duty but about to take his lunch break. They were alone in the employee's tiny break room. The opening question was asking Doug to tell them everything he knew about Doreen, Andrew and Dolly.

"I knew Andrew from high school. He was always a party animal. Everyone I know wrote in

Andrew's yearbook that he should cut back on the drinking. We lost touch for a while when Andrew was away at college, but when he returned, I would invite him to my parties a few times a year. Andrew isn't someone I would hang out with on a regular basis. Besides the heavy drinking, he was very vocal during football games. One night at a bar, we almost had to fight our way out and were told by the owner to never come back. I decided to only see him in private homes after that. After being banned from my favorite bar, I was complaining to Dolly about it. I told her that Andrew was a good guy in some ways, like working hard and acting like a gentleman, but drinking was not a good thing for him.

When I had my next party, I invited Dolly to come. I could tell she was interested in meeting Andrew, and she knew that he and his girlfriend had just broken up. I wasn't too keen on the idea, but since Dolly doesn't drink at all, maybe if Andrew was interested in Dolly, it would help him straighten out. Dolly called that night and said her sister wanted to come, so I said the more the merrier. Dolly tried to appear coy about her interest in Andrew, but was working the room in his direction. Doreen made a bee-line for Andrew and threw herself at him. She worked the body and face like everything he said was so important. By the time Dolly walked over to join the conversation, it was too late. I don't know if Doreen knew Dolly was interested in Andrew and deliberately blocked her out of malice, or if she cut her out by accident, but Dolly sure was hurt. She ignored them the rest of the night and tried to talk to other guys, but I know her well enough to see how upset she was.

After the Andrew and Doreen relationship took off, Dolly would talk about how rude he would be to Doreen and to her. She would say if Doreen wanted that kind of life, it was up to her but she was glad she didn't get him. I doubt she was sincere. Most guys don't get past the weight issue to see what a sweet girl Dolly really is. I only saw Doreen about three times at parties and really had limited conversations with her. Andrew was into the relationship so much, he limited times with friends so I didn't see him much either.

Do you think it was an accident? About Doreen, I mean. How is Andrew taking it? I called once and left a voicemail saying how sorry I was to hear about what happened, but he never returned the call so I thought he just wanted to be left alone."

Jessie fielded questions about Doreen with the standard reply. "We don't know. That's why we are asking questions to be sure." She suggested that Andrew might be more receptive to a call since a few weeks had passed, but that was up to Doug. As they exited the facility, they could see Dolly coming out of the manager's office and she froze in her tracks.

Jessie walked over to say hello in a very friendly manner. "We are just finishing up on our inquires and would like to talk to you again when you have time."

"Not now, I just got to work and don't want to get into trouble," Dolly said looking over her shoulder at the office door.

Jessie persisted, "When are you off work?"

"Not until 11:00 tonight and off all day tomorrow. It won't do any good to talk again. I told you all I know." The worried look didn't leave Dolly's face as she spoke.

Jessie smiled, "Just trying to do right for your sister by checking thoroughly. We will come by your place in the morning. See you then."

The next stop was the best man's office. Russ was on the phone cutting deals and sweet-talking customers as he motioned the detectives to the chairs in front of his desk. Russ got off the phone as quickly as he could, then he turned his attention to the visitors, "What's happening?"

James led off the conversation. The detectives found man-to-man and woman-to-woman interviews often produced the best results unless the man appeared interested in Detective Johnson, then James would fade into the background as much as possible. Russ appeared to be a happy husband and dad so not even a sideways glance went to Jessie. "We are still checking into the Doreen case and wondered if you had any more information that might be helpful."

Russ spread his hands apart, "I told you everything I know about that night. I don't think it was helpful, but it was honest."

James continued, "Maybe not information about that night but information about the relationship Doreen had with others, like maybe her family."

Russ was very smart and picked up on where the conversation was going, "No, I never met her family before that night. My wife didn't like Doreen, and honestly, neither did I. We felt Andrew could do much better, but we have been best friends for years, and so we made getting together a buddy thing and not a couple's time. My wife and I have small children. We always used them as an excuse for me to get together with Andrew while she watched the kids, and she would make an excuse to be gone with me watching the kids if Andrew came over. My wife really had reservations about Andrew but knew not to get between friends."

James questioned, "Did Andrew ever talked

about Doreen's family to you? Even though it would be hearsay, it might prove helpful."

"Andrew said that Maria was nice at first, but then he realized it was an act. He said Dolly was always grumpy around him so he avoided her. He said Donna made a pass at him once. While he was flattered, he didn't think it would be a good idea. Andrew felt that Donna made a pass at every man in the room. The dad and him got along good. When Doreen and Andrew visited her family, Andrew would always ask about something outside in the yard or garage so the two men could get out of the house and avoid the women. He said Doreen complained about her family regularly, especially the way her mom treated her, but would ask if they could go over and hang out with them. Andrew was trying to cut back on the time with Doreen's family by having lots of plans for them, but it was a touchy situation. I know Doreen didn't like me either, but we could fake being nice for an evening for the sake of Andrew."

Back in the car heading for the third interview of the day, James and Jessie agreed that the earlier interviews with the family, in which all professed total love and commitment to Doreen, might have been either the impact of the sorrow or to hide the real tension between the sisters. Maria's determination to have either Andrew or Norma in trouble for her daughter's death might lead to some surprising and unwanted results.

Going back to Maria's for more questions was something they both dreaded. Maria greeted them at the door with an angry attitude. "Why are those horrible people not in jail for hurting my precious little girl? Why don't you want to do your job?"

Jessie took a deep breath to calm her nerves before saying, "We have no evidence there was a murder or that Norma or Andrew did anything wrong. We wondered about Doreen's home life and how she interacted with her family and friends."

"GET OUT! GET OUT NOW! How dare you come into our grieving home and act like there was anything wrong within our loving, wonderful, God-fearing family! I will be talking to your superiors and get you fired."

James stepped up saying, "No one said your family did anything wrong. We wondered if you talked about or knew anything about Doreen's friends or old boyfriends."

"None of her friends or old boyfriends were there! Go after the two I told you to!" James and Jessie left knowing there was no point in further conversation.

The last stop of the day was at Donna's place of employment. The two detectives were greeted at the door by her boss. The boss said Donna didn't want to talk with them and they would need to leave. It appeared Maria already called and told the family that no one was supposed to talk to James and Jessie. Being on private property and at her work, they didn't have the right to push for an interview.

"What do we do next?" the less experienced Jessie asked her partner.

"I guess we need to go back to Norma and see if we can get another lead." James knew his partner was against him seeing Norma again, so he suggested she join them.

He called and Norma said "It's Friday night. I am going out with David and his wife, but you two can join us." She gave them an address and time. "It's a dress-up occasion like tux or suits for men and formals for ladies."

Jessie was less than happy with the arrangement, "Taking my Friday night and having to dress up so uncomfortable? That is above and beyond the call of duty."

Chapter 30 - The Dance

The address ended up being a dance studio but unlike one that James or Jessie ever saw. They walked into a reception hall which was lit with crystal chandeliers and containing a glass and chrome desk. A beautiful lady with a flowing gown, hair swept on top of her head, and covered with rhinestone jewelry greeted them. "Norma said she had guests coming. Is this your first ballroom experience?"

Both detectives gave a gulp, but it was James that sputtered out the word yes. Jessie was too busy looking back at the exit and trying to decide if she should run away. Jessie was a master of walking up to a gang of troublemakers and handling it just fine, but this genteel world was not in her comfort level. The lady lead them down a hallway that had doors closed on each side. She pointed out the facilities, her word for the restrooms, and at the end of the hall, they entered a huge room lined with mirrors and numerous crystal chandeliers overhead. Tables lined the outer walls, including a banquet table with food and a crystal punch bowl set and glasses.

Jessie leaned over and whispered, "Did we travel to another universe?"

Norma waved and walked over to greet them. She looked so beautiful dressed in a red V-necked dress with long sleeves that glittered under the lights and with the skirt swirling as she stepped. Jessie felt awkward realizing the feminine beauty and grace that Norma possessed.

"I'm so glad you could come. Why don't you get a glass of punch, not spiked of course, or water before you join us?" Walking to the table, Norma explained that alcohol interferes with the timing of the dancers and that a person certainly didn't need to drink to have fun. The 'us' she was referring to was David and his wife, Beth, who was sitting in a wheelchair.

"Do you dance?" inquired David. Both James and Jessie responded no but their hesitant manner didn't dampen Dave's enthusiastic attitude. "You'll love it. It is very addicting to enjoy the movement and flow."

Jessie looked at the many dancers on the floor

that were smiling, laughing, and flowing around the room. David took her hand and invited her to join him. "Not just yet. Let me watch for a bit and see if I can get the idea of being out there and not running someone over."

David and Norma walked onto the floor and began waltzing around the room. They appeared to know everyone, speaking as they passed, laughing and enjoying the fun. Jessie looked over at Beth who had such a forlorn expression. As soon as Beth realized Jessie was looking at her, she forced a smile onto her face, "I was a very good dancer, but this accident left me on the sideline. I can't take the fun away from my husband, who is one of the best dancers out there. I'm grateful that Norma agreed to partner with him and tries to make me a part of the events, but I still miss being on the floor."

James' total attention turned to Beth. She started giving him instructions on the steps. She pointed out couples that were newer to dancing that still counted out the steps so it would be easier for Jessie and James to get the idea of how to move. It was evident that Beth was a true expert on the subject.

Norma and David returned, standing over James and Jessie commanding, "Let's go out there now." James took Norma's hand and while he enjoyed the walk onto the floor, he dreaded the next part. David was expertly leading Jessie around the room, but James didn't know how to lead in a dance. After stepping on Norma's foot a couple of times, Norma and David led James and Jessie down the hall and into one of the rooms behind the closed door. Beth wheeled along behind.

David started the instructions on the basic steps with Norma helping him demonstrate. Then the experts paired with the two new students and they started doing the steps they had just watched. Jessie was ok on the movements but was dancing like a straight pole with no flow or gentle movement of the hips. First, Norma demonstrated and had Jessie try to do the steps with a graceful, sexy shift of the weight. Next, Norma danced with David and told Jessie to put her hands on Norma's hips then copy the movement with her own. The third and final attempt was with Jessie dancing with David and Norma trying to shift Jessie's hips.

James sat with Beth laughing out loud. The usually totally-in-control Jessie was like a scared child. Finally, Jessie turned with her hands on her hips and temper showing on her face. "What does this have to do with the investigation?"

James tried to curtail the laughing but couldn't remove his huge grin.

Norma intervened, "Jessie, why don't you try laughing? You can't be stiff and tight when you're laughing. Come on and try, ha ha ha ha." The tone of the laugh was like singing the scales, and even Jessie had to laugh at Norma's silliness. After an hour of practice and with helpful suggestions from Beth, they were ready to re-enter the foreign world called the ballroom. This time their movements were not smooth, but at least David and Norma wouldn't get as many crushed toes.

A romantic mood flowed through James as he glided to the music with the lovely Norma in his arms. "I would love to learn more and do this again sometime."

Norma smiled because she enjoyed being wrapped in the strong arms of James. "Maybe next time, I'll even let you lead."

The dancing went on for hours with David and Norma performing the harder dances like the tango and the rumba. James loved it when songs were played that he could dance the waltz or the East coast swing to. He got his turn on the dance floor and didn't want to sit down. Even Jessie was starting to have a good time, with only a slight improvement on the dance moves.

Beth whispered to Norma and the two wheeled down the hall to the restroom. James was a little embarrassed for Beth but when she returned, she put his mind to ease saying, "Now that is a true friend."

Once on the dance floor, he asked Norma about Beth's limitations. Norma said, "No one likes to get or give help in something so simple as meeting Mother Nature's needs but you do what is needed for your friends." His respect for Norma went up even more. Here she looked so lovely on the outside, but the caring and compassion she displayed for her mother and Beth made her lovely on the inside too.

Needing a break from dancing, the party of five went onto the patio for some fresh air. Surprisingly, Norma brought up the case by asking if they found out any further information on Doreen's family. Jessie was silent, thinking it wasn't proper to discuss the case even though she really didn't consider Norma a suspect at this time. James told everything of the interviews of the previous few days. When he related Maria's outburst claiming what a 'good God-fearing family' they were, Norma tried to suppress a laugh, but David's laugh was very loud.

"You could have fooled me," he said. "I only saw her the night of the wedding, but I never saw anyone with less joy. Being a Christian myself, I believe in being happy. I'm going to tell you something that is very unchristian on my part, and it was on Maria's part too. At the end of the wedding, the mother of the bride wore a silver, very tight dress with a peek-a-boo in the cleavage area and got on the dance floor with her husband. All other couples were dancing like normal, facing each other, but not Maria. She stuck her behind into her husband's crotch and he dangled his hands over her shoulders. They were out just from her breasts, but at least he didn't squeeze them. He stood there while she moved and rubbed herself on him. It was a lap dance with clothes on if you ask me. I don't see how anyone could profess to be so spiritual when you treat your guests so rudely, pit your daughters against each other, dress like a slut, and lap dance at your daughter's wedding."

Norma only added in a quiet voice, "It really was that bad. He's not overstating the truth."

Beth just said, "I wish I could have been there to see it." Everyone laughed but with a little sadness at the situation being so negative.

James said he tried to follow up with interviews with the two remaining daughters, but the whole family quit speaking to the police. Donna and Maria called in sick, but Dolly's boss said she took all her vacation time and sick time as a leave of absence, claiming she was too upset over the death of her sister to work for a few weeks. Maria called the detective's supervisor to complain about James and Jessie's behavior, but at least their boss backed them, saying Maria wanted an investigation and that was exactly what they were doing.

Norma asked if all the cars were in the driveway at Maria's home. James recalled he didn't see Dolly's but it might have been behind the garage.

The discussion put a damper on the evening so David and Beth left. James and Jessie drove Norma to her house and Norma invited them in for further discussion.

Chapter 31 - Knowledge is not Proof

Daniel and his girlfriend were in the family room so Norma suggested drinks in the formal living room. Jessie was not a drinker so she settled on grape juice, while Norma and James opened a bottle of red wine. After the appropriate comments about the lovely room and house, Norma was ready to get down to business.

"This has gone on long enough. I need to know what was used to kill Doreen," Norma said.

It was almost a command instead of a question. Again, Jessie was reluctant to answer the question, as she wanted to be asking the questions instead. However, James didn't hesitate, "It was a mixture of Oxycodone combined with the vodka that did it."

Norma sat there like the detective she loved to read about in the Rex Stout mysteries with her eyes closed and deep in thought for a few minutes. James looked at Jessie and both shrugged their shoulders. They didn't know if she was asleep or if they should break her concentration.

Finally, Norma opened her eyes and said, "I'm going to tell you one more story. I was summoned to the bridal store by Doreen. She claimed it was a request, but like all of our other encounters, it was very planned. Maria and Doreen were there when I arrived. They showed me three dresses they picked out for me to choose from that were approved for me to wear. All looked like something an old lady would wear: dark, drab, loose, and no flow to the skirts for someone to dance in. They were very over-priced for the poor quality of the dress. I tried them on out of obligation and didn't like any of them. The bridal store is set up with a row of changing rooms in an L-shape. Along the back wall, there are about six rooms, and then around the corner are three rooms by the alteration department. I was coming out of one of the rooms facing the store while Maria and Doreen were in the two rooms around the corner. Doreen was standing on a stool and the seamstress was working on her gown length.

Dolly came in the front door and walked over to me to say hello. Maria and Doreen could not see she was there and Doreen was too busy talking to hear us speak. Doreen told her mother 'Can't you make Dolly lose some weight before the wedding? She's so fat that it will ruin an otherwise perfect wedding.'

Maria said 'That's not nice. She is your sister and you should be happy she is there for you.' Maria was saying the right words but her tone of voice showed that she was laughing and thought it was funny. Dolly wasn't really that fat. She was a little overweight, but not with rolls of fat. She was sensitive about her size so they often used that as an attack.

Tears filled Dolly's eyes as she leaned over and whispered, 'Please don't tell them I was here,' and she turned and walked out. I should have said more but it happened so fast, and actually I was shocked at the cruel attitude of both Maria and Doreen.

At the bridal shower, Dolly came over and said hello and asked me if I was excited about the wedding. I was honest and said no, but if that is what my son wanted, I would have to live with it. She squeezed my hand and walked away."

James and Jessie both sat staring for a few minutes. Jessie was the first to say what they all thought, "I guess you can only push a person so far. Do you think Dolly hit the limit of what she could bear?"

Again, another long pause then Norma called

Daniel over and asked him to join them. Daniel and his girlfriend entered while Norma refreshed their drinks. James started to protest that he had to drive but honestly felt he would like another. "Daniel, will you please tell James and Jessie about the night of the furniture move?"

Daniel sat down and looked into their faces as he talked. "Mom was out with friends from the gym for the night, and I was supposed to go stay with my grandmother. Mom agreed to let Andrew have the dresser and bed from the back room. Andrew had a key so I was about to leave when he called. He was already in route and forgot the key because he left it on the key rack by the door. He asked me to stay until they arrived and moved the furniture. Mom said to leave the house clean because she was sure that Maria would want a full report of the house when they got home. I really didn't trust any of them, truth be told. I didn't like the fact that people were going to enter our house when Mom and I weren't there so I decided to mark the doors to the bedrooms, bathrooms, and every closet.

I had trouble when I rented an apartment one time and didn't trust the landlord, so I learned to mark the door so I could tell if he entered while I was gone. Each room had two markings, one at the top and a hair at the handle. When the group arrived, there was not only Andrew and the dad, but

Doreen, Maria and Dolly were in the truck. The women went into the family room and sat down. The two men went to the back bedroom to take the bed apart and to decide how they were going to load the things in the truck. It took an unusually long time for them to do the work. Maria and Dolly both decided they needed to go to the bathroom at the same time. Maria went into the one by the door to my mother's bedroom and Dolly went to the one in the back bedroom where the men were working. After they returned to the front room, I went in and looked. The closets and medicine cabinets of both rooms had been opened. In other words, the place had been searched."

Norma walked over and handed the two detectives rubber gloves. "I have these from when the nursing staff would come to the house to work on Mom. We will need a pretty big evidence bag. Let's go back and get what I fear might be the murder weapon." The three walked to the back bathroom and Norma opened the door. Inside was a shoebox filled with about three dozen prescription bottles, "One of those bottles contains Oxycodone, but I don't know which one. Mom took care of her own medicine when she lived here. I would bring the box to her and she would fill up her pill boxes for morning and night. I'm very opposed to drugs and had no interest in helping her with her medicine. Most of the health problems that mom had were caused by the use of prescribed drugs. My fingerprints would be on the edges of the box, but I'm not sure they would be on the pill bottles. Even if I did touch them, Mom would have touched them after me. I talked to Daniel, and he said that he never touched the containers either."

James put on the gloves and while reaching for the shoebox asked, "Can we take the whole box?"

"Yes."

"Do you know how many pills were in the bottle before and what number should be there now?"

"No."

"How long have the pills been in there?"

"Three years."

"How often and how long did your mother use this drug?"

"She only had that prescription filled one time. She didn't like the effects of the drug on her. She would have hallucinations so she only took those pills a couple of times, I think."

"Did Andrew know the drugs were here? Do you have any clue if he would have mentioned the drugs to anyone?"

"To my knowledge, Andrew didn't know the

drugs were in the house and neither did Daniel until just now."

"Do you have any further knowledge that we should know about the murder or the time of Dolly being in the house?"

"No."

"I wonder if Dolly is on the run and if so, where would she go?" Jessie disliked asking questions that sounded like asking for help, but Norma did seem to have all the answers.

"I would ask Doug because I think he was the only one she trusted. But if I had to guess, I would say Dolly would go to her father's house."

James turned looking surprised, "Why would she go to the man that deserted her as a child and left her with such an evil person?"

Again, the observant Norma had her logic, "When Andrew contacted Juan, he seemed very interested in connecting with his daughters, but told Andrew he hadn't because of Maria's threats to have him put in jail. Andrew explained that the statutes of limitation were expired, and since he had no contact with the family that she couldn't do anything to him now. Juan was still hesitant because he felt so bad about leaving his girls, but Andrew told him that the only way to ever have a relationship was to come forward. When Maria sent

Dolly down to order Juan away from the wedding, she wasn't angry but hopeful, even happy to speak to him. Juan understood that his ex-wife would be watching and trying to find fault. He told Dolly to act angry and to order him away with her gestures, but in reality they had a brief, but nice talk. Andrew and I both watched every move to see what would happen. I saw Juan slip a paper into Dolly's hand. I'm sure no one else saw it. Dolly spent her whole life being mentally abused by the whole family, especially by Maria. Even though she was of age, she never left the home. She had no confidence in herself and was afraid that if she left and had to come back, it would be even worse because she would be labeled a failure, so she just stayed living in misery. Juan slipping her that paper, no doubt inviting her to call, might have been the opening she needed for her escape. I have to wonder, if it was Dolly that did this, you have to wonder if she was meaning to kill Doreen or just ruin her wedding night."

That was the end to what had been a pleasant evening. Norma walked them to the door and said goodnight. James assured her he would call soon.

Chapter 32 – Answers

It was three days before Norma heard from James. He called as she was driving to the nursing home to see what her plans were for the evening. "I've just picked up a pizza and we plan to have dinner on the patio tonight. Do you want to join us?"

When James arrived, Betty's back was to him. He mouthed, "Should I talk in front of her?" Norma shook her head no. James greeted the two ladies with a kiss on the cheek and a hug. Betty was always thrilled when James was there. She inquired about the case and James just said that he would fill them in when he could and that Norma would probably let her know instead of him. The talk was light and fun about a new television show on dancing and about James' dancing progress. A nurse's aide came to the patio and asked if dinner was over so she could give Betty her bath and get her ready for bed. Norma told her mother to go ahead and that she would wait on the patio. Norma assured her that she would say good night after she was comfortably in bed.

The minute that the door was shut to the building, James knew Norma wanted explanations immediately by her eager look. "I'm sorry I didn't get back to you sooner but things have really been busy. The medicine bottles were checked for fingerprints. It looked like someone used a towel or a cloth to lift each bottle because their lids were wiped clean only on one side of the top. The exception was the bottle with the Oxycodone, which was wiped clean altogether. It was only about half full, which didn't match what you thought your mother had used.

The next day, Jessie and I went to Maria's again and threatened to take her to jail as a material witness if she and the family didn't talk to us. Only after a call to the station to find out that we had the right to do what we were threatening did she finally let us into the house. In the corner of the room was a small table made into a shrine. There was a large cross, a picture of Doreen, a single rose in a bud vase, and a couple of candles. Maria had no clue where Dolly was, but Donna was there.

We talked to Donna alone over Maria's

objections, but with Donna being an adult, Maria couldn't stop us. Donna said Maria was going about the house acting like Doreen had been a saint and almost worshiping her. Everything Dolly and Donna did was put down with the phrase, 'Your sister wouldn't have done it that way.' Donna thought maybe Dolly ran away because the pressure was getting to everyone, even Maria's loving husband. Donna said she was moving in with her new boyfriend this weekend so she could get away herself.

Donna felt sure when Dolly went to the party it was with the intent to attract Andrew's attention. Dolly felt Doreen had squeezed her out of the picture intentionally. In fact, Doreen was proud of the maneuver and had bragged about it behind Dolly's back. Donna kept repeating that Dolly was a good person and wouldn't hurt anyone. We didn't say anything about Dolly possibly being involved, but I think the family is concerned that it was her. At least we feel they know something that they aren't telling us. We tried to call Juan and Dolly's cell phones, but didn't get an answer or a return call from either of them.

Afterwards, we went to see Doug. We told him we needed to talk to Dolly. He said he hadn't seen her since she took her vacation time. We told him that we knew he was the only one Dolly trusted and assured him we wanted to help her. We asked if she went to her father's and Doug showed a reaction.

'Don't you ever tell Maria,' he said, 'She is so mean to Dolly, she might hunt her down.' We assured him we were under no obligation to tell Maria. He believed us and confirmed that Juan did slip his number to Dolly at the wedding and told her how sorry he was for leaving her. Juan had assured Dolly that he would be there for her if she ever wanted to contact him. Dolly had called and told him about Maria's forcing them to worship Doreen and she had to get away. Juan begged her to come and to trust him. Both Juan and Dolly knew it was better for Maria not to know. It was hard to say what evil thing she would do.

We drove the three hours to Juan's house. His wife and children were there. They told us that Dolly was so glad to be staying in their home, even though she was still plagued with nightmares. After a few days, she was exhausted and shaking so badly, it was hard for her to drink from a cup without a straw. At this point, they thought it might be drug withdrawals, but Dolly assured them that she never did drugs. Finally, Dolly asked if they knew of a place she could go to get mental help. She felt like she was having a nervous breakdown. After hearing the stories of her life, they promised to help her and stand by her. Dolly is now residing in a very nice institution by her own choice.

We went and saw the place and it is very bright and cheerful. We talked to her doctor but were not permitted to interview Dolly. We told him our suspicions but he is well-versed in the law and would not say anything that would violate a confidence. He also pointed out what we already knew, that we haven't found a shred of evidence. He thanked us for the information and assured me that Dolly was in good hands.

Our boss and the D.A. decided the case would go into the unsolved case file. I think that is the best thing too. Over 40 percent of the murders in the United States go unsolved not because we don't know who the murderer was, but sometimes we just don't have the evidence, like in this case.

Why didn't you become a detective, Norma? I understand you have helped out on cases often in the past and that you're good at it."

Norma reached out and took James' hand, "I couldn't bear to see what you witness all the time, the violence and negative side of humans. I'm not tough and brave with confidence like Jessie. You two face so much, I'm glad you have someone like Jessie to lean on and back you up."

They went in and kissed Betty goodnight and left.

James said, "I want to go somewhere for another half hour or so because there is something else I feel I need to tell you. I want to go somewhere you don't ever visit because after what I have to tell you, I assure you that you won't want to go there again."

They stopped at a pub down the street. James ordered coffee for himself and a drink for Norma. "Trying to get me drunk so you can arrest me, officer?"

James laughed and responded, "If you got drunk, I would take you home, not to jail."

Norma then stated seriously, "I take it you're going to say something about Andrew."

James wondered how she seemed to know things. "Yes, I talked to Andrew but couldn't tell him that we suspected Dolly. While we went to ask Andrew about Dolly and Doreen's relationship, he said he always suspected it was someone from Doreen's family because he knew he was innocent, and that you would never do anything to hurt someone on purpose. He knew how cutthroat the family was and thought that by marrying Doreen, he might have been able to save her. He does still blame you for her death, though."

Norma's voice had a very upset edge to it. "How could he? I thought you just said he knew I would never do something like that." Tears were in her eyes but she refused to let them flow.

James reached out to hold Norma's hand, "Your ex-husband told Andrew since you were so good at solving murders, that surely you were smart enough to see one coming and you could have prevented it if you hadn't disliked Doreen so much."

James continued as the tears flowed from Norma's eyes. "I was very angry and yelled at Andrew that wasn't logical. I told him you would have stopped it if you knew it was coming but how could you have known? He had no answer but stuck by his asinine conclusion."

Norma's voice was shaking and her tears were flowing, but she was very quiet. "If I was that smart, I wouldn't have been so stupid as to enter into the marriage that created him. I was naïve enough to believe that the love and goodness I tried to show my son would win over the lies and evil words of my ex-husband."

James moved over to the other side of the booth so he could sit with his arms around Norma. The silence lasted a long time. Finally, James decided it was time to move on. "Norma, you are a wonderful person. I only know two people that dislike you, your ex-husband and your son. Andrew's dislike is only because of the poison he was fed all those years. Andrew is smart enough to see it in Maria and Doreen, but can't apply it to his own life because he would have to realize his father is bad before he could see that you are good."

Norma kissed James and said, "You are right. Now I never want to come back here again."

James laughed and walked Norma to her car. "Are you ok to drive? I don't mean from the drink, but from the shock."

Norma assured him that she was ok. "I'll be doing a lot of praying on the way home because that's the only way I can find peace in all this."

"Can we go dancing Friday night again?" James asked, smiling in a boyish way.

"Yes, but you better watch out for Beth. I think she is playing matchmaker."

They kissed again and James replied, "Let her."

Chapter 33 - A Beginning

James and Norma continued the routine of visiting Betty, dinner during the week when he could get away, and dancing on the weekends for a few weeks. After James relayed the comment Norma made to the brave and courageous Jessie, she was playing matchmaker too, but she wasn't ready to go dancing again. Norma told James there was no dance this coming Friday night, so James asked if she would be willing to work with him on his dance moves at her house. Norma said she would like that. Daniel was going with his girlfriend to her parent's beach house, so the music wouldn't disturb the young couple.

James arrived to find Norma dressed in a white flowing ball gown with pleated chiffon sleeves so she looked like an angel.

He presented Norma with a bottle of red wine.

"I know we aren't supposed to drink while we dance but there's no one here to see us make mistakes."

James put on a rumba, his new favorite dance, and then a waltz. James lifted their glasses and they toasted to endings and new beginnings. As Norma poured another glass for them, James pulled a CD from his pocket and slipped the disc in the player and pressed number 7.

"I want to see what moves you suggest for this song." The Moody Blues 'Nights in White Satin' began to play while James took Norma into his arms. James could feel Norma's tension and her reluctance to dance.

After a minute, James stopped and looked very seriously into Norma's eyes. "Look, I prefer things to happen naturally and not control the situation by talking too much, but that isn't going to work in this case. I hope I don't screw this up like I have in the past with you, Norma. You remind me of a horse that knows the barn door is open and is about to make a break for it." *Shit*, he thought, *I should have used a bird-in-a-cage analogy. I just insinuated she is a horse.*

"I understand the mistreatment you have endured from your ex-husband and son, and while I can't promise everything will be perfect, I can promise I will never mistreat you. I didn't meet you and say, 'I want to have sex with her.' I saw you and felt peacefulness, a calmness come over me. You are someone I want to be with as a partner in life, to share experiences and walk with. I want you to be my friend and my anchor. From these feelings comes my desire to be passionate with you. I don't want to push you and I'm willing to take it slow, but please don't shut me out and run because of your fear that the past will be repeated.

You told me the story of the dog on the front porch, and if you recall, I was sitting on your front doorstep when you came home that day. You accepted the dog into your life because even if it isn't what you wanted, you knew it was what God had planned. I really feel I'm a part of that plan now."

Norma reached up and kissed James with so much passion that he could feel it head to toe. *Oh good*, thought James, *maybe she didn't pick up on the error of his earlier comparison.*

After a couple of kisses, Norma assumed her dance posture and they started swaying to the music. "You are right. I feel that completeness too when we are together. Maybe you are what I need to make me heal from the hurt I had in the past. I'm willing to overlook that I'm a horse, and that you are the dog on my doorstep, and move forward from here."

There was a look on her face that he could tell she was trying not to laugh. *Ok I didn't get away with it*, thought James, *but at least she is taking it with the good intentions I intended.*

"I really find it hard to believe you're a detective at times, Mr. Murphy. Do you woo all your murder suspects with such flattery?"

They both laughed. "No, Norma, I'm only tongue-tied around you." The dancing continued but with broken frame as they held each other close. "You do realize, after 20 years of being alone, that we might not survive the weekend," said Norma.

James was now smiling. "I'm willing to take that chance." The dance was like something James had never experienced before. Emotions intensified as they moved to the music and later to the bedroom.

On Monday, when James picked up Jessie for work, he was happy and singing a little off-key.

Jessie smiled, "What happened to that grumpy, depressed man I use to work with? I'm glad to see the new, happier you."

James said while smiling, "That grump is in 'Days of Future Past'."

Jessie looked at James like he was out of his mind. *I guess this is another question that only*

Norma could find the answer to, she thought with a smiled.

Until Next Time

It was another lovely day on the porch in the rockers for the group of friends. All were silent considering the elements of the story they just heard. Josephine was the only one with no questions because she knew the story firsthand.

Eve had a curious look on her face. "I don't understand the 'Days of Future Past' comment."

Belinda said, "Don't you remember? That was the title of the Moody Blues album in which the song 'Nights in White Satin' was a huge hit. Besides, if I guess correctly, besides the song title, James Murphy changed from a lonely, not necessarily cheerful person to one full of joy, right?"

Jean nodded yes.

"Also if I guess right, could James be your

longtime boyfriend who is a detective in Forest City?"

No comment or head shake was given by Jean, who tried as hard as she could to hide the little smile that came to her lips. "No comment, but I can't help but think of Nick without a smile coming to my lips."

Priscilla asked, "Why haven't you and Nick ever married? Do you think you will someday?"

Josephine laughed, "You saw her reaction to someone else's wedding. I would hate to see how she would act at her own."

Jean just smiled, "Things are perfect the way they are now. Why take a chance of ruining a good thing?" Jean was a little older than Nick who was still working full-time. "There is less pressure on Nick with his odd hours at work. It is better for him not having a wife to hurry home to. This way, we are together when it is good for both of us, not because we are living in the same house."

Jean was also thinking that she liked having her own space as well as sleeping alone. The truth was Nick and Jean both snored sometimes, and it disturbed the non-snoring partner. This way, either one could get up and go to the other's home since it was only about 15 minutes down the road. However, since she considered this personal and none of the ladies' business, it was left unsaid.

"When do we start another story?" asked Eve.

Jean responded, "In a couple of days. I might need time to make up some more." Jean was thinking that next time she would choose one that didn't hurt her heart when it was told.

Priscilla looked up as if reading Jean's thoughts, "Do you think Andrew was ever sorry about being so mean to Norma? Do you think they ever solved their differences?"

Jean, not wanting to admit what parts of the story were true and what parts were false, selected her words carefully, "I think the point to take from that relationship is that you can't make someone love you. You can't make someone see the truth, and you can't make someone be nice to you. All you can do is respect their desire to withdraw from your life. My guess, if I was to write another chapter, but I won't, it would be about Andrew regretting his ways but being too proud to make things right. I have doubts that he would ever be able to see the truth and the mistakes he made. I believe he would make up his own truth about the events of the story and not acknowledge what really happened.

The moral to this story is that negativity destroys. In this story, the negative Maria destroyed all three of her daughters, especially Dolly and Doreen, and ended up alone in her misery. Andrew's father used his hatred of Norma to hurt her by destroying his own son. I hear people say that to be a parent, you should have to take an IQ test, but the truth is, the test needs to be one of compassion, love, and wisdom, which doesn't always mean intelligence.

A second moral is to live life happy, no matter what your circumstances are. Having a positive attitude and being grateful for your blessing will open the door for good things to come into your life, even something as unexpected as true love."

ABOUT THE AUTHOR

Mia Tenroc started reading mysteries when she was 12 years old, Rex Stout and Agatha Christie being her favorites. She and her sister vowed to  become mystery writers. Unable to work together, Mia designed the series with central characters that introduce each story in the first chapter but then each book is its own story. That way, she and her sister could write their own stories yet use these characters as the connection.

Mia's books are dedicated to demonstrating how what we say to one another really matters. She hopes to show that kind words build self-esteem and elevates people. A dedicated people watcher, Mia observes families interacting with each other which she uses as the basis for her books.

Mia tries to incorporate her small town into the books because there is a great joy in knowing your neighbors and being surrounded by family and friends. Mia loves to travel and experience the fun of seeing new place.

ORDERING INFORMATION

To get copies of this and other books by Mia Tenroc, please contact:

McToner Publishing Inc.
P.O. Box 37
Goldenrod, Florida 32722
McTonerPublishing@gmail.com
www.Miatenroc.com